CONTENTS

The Existence Of Amy

By Lana Grace Riva

Chapter 1

I register the light before anything else. No thoughts yet, no feelings, just light. Light is usually a symbol of hope, yet at this very second, it's distorted into disappointment. It guides to my first thought of the day – 'I'm still here'. Still a live human being fumbling to cope with existence.

I keep my eyes closed a little while longer. Almost in the hope I might be mistaken. Perhaps this is actually what happens next and I've passed in my sleep. But of course, I know that's not the case. I've got another day of facing it.

I raise myself up and sit on the side of my bed for some time. I don't know why I do this. All it really does is prolong things, but it feels like I need this step. I need to stay in contact with my bed for these last few minutes of vague comfort before it all starts.

Eventually I get up and accept it has begun.

I have a shower. I get dressed. I have breakfast. I get my things ready to leave. This all takes quite a large amount of time because... well, this will become apparent soon enough. For now, it's safe to say that my 'getting ready' time is far from in alignment with what would be deemed average. Even to what would be deemed above average. It is in no way connected to average.

After a somewhat exhausting, frustrating and irritating time I eventually find myself standing in front of the door and pause for one last moment before leaving. I search for some instruction and cling to it when it appears. 'You can do this'. 'Don't listen to those other thoughts, you are stronger than them'. 'You can absolutely do this'.

Can I though? It's very much debatable.

I step outside in the knowledge that the worst is yet to come.

It's always worse outside. My home could perhaps be described as my 'safe space'. However, I would venture that a far more accurate description would be that my home is my 'safest space possible to achieve without actually feeling all that safe'.

The first challenge I am tasked with is my journey to work.

I work in an office that is unfortunately not walking distance from my home. I don't own a car, nor do I even drive, so the only option I am left with is to use public transport. Given I have to work to pay my bills I conclude I must face this option or face being unable to afford my home.

For the majority of the time my brain correctly calculates which side should win in this battle between facing public transport and facing losing my job. Unfortunately, however, not all the time.

Today thankfully I am feeling able to tackle this.

As I stand waiting for the bus to arrive, I try to search for some kind of calm that I can persuade to accompany me on the journey. Sometimes I can catch a glimpse of it, but it always seems just beyond my reach. Not near enough to make it worth even attempting persuading discussion.

I am at least a little fortunate today in that the bus arrives not long after I reach the stop. Waiting time equates to thinking time and I need less of both if I am to be successful.

As soon as I step on the bus, I immediately embark on scanning the options as fast as I can. There is substantially limited time for this, so I know I must use it wisely.

It's rush hour, the busiest time of day, so there's a long line of passengers waiting behind me. It's obvious they are feeling not such their patient selves. I don't know whether they're desperate to get to work, or desperate for the journey there to be over. Perhaps they're in a similar state of distress as myself but it seems quite unlikely. Whatever their reasons, the result is an unpleasant atmosphere of vast grumpiness.

Anyone taking slightly longer then an arbitrary acceptable time to find a seat and sit down will likely be met with loud sighing and/ or tutting. In addition to this they will be gifted with an assumption that they are impolite, inconsiderate, and a generally horrible person for holding up the bus.

I don't want this assumption labelled onto me but neither do I want to raise my level of discomfort at being on this bus any higher than it's already at. So, I carry out my scanning as quickly as I possibly can and hope I make the best choice for which seat to sit in.

Today I perhaps wasn't quick enough. It really is a difficult thing to get right. I have selected an aisle seat but unfortunately its adjoining window seat is currently empty. I read the expression on the passenger to alight behind me – 'Well that was lovely and selfish of you wasn't it – hoping to spread out over two seats were you?'.

I desperately want to answer them. To defend myself. It's hard though to answer when you are both transmitting messages only in silence. How can I form a look on my face that will read 'I'm not intentionally being selfish, I promise! I just have this thing... and I can't...'. My answer wouldn't be sufficient anyway – it's not something easily summed up in a few apologetic sentences.

Instead I avert my gaze from their face and let their scorn carve through me.

A few minutes pass when someone inevitably stops next to my seat asking if they can sit in the window seat. I get up to let them in and they smile at me. I say a silent 'thank you' because they seem like a relatively acceptable bus seat neighbour. The main criteria for this being that they keep within the space of their own seat and don't allow any of their body parts to touch any of mine.

The fact they smiled at me offers some small relief too. They can't have been too offended at my aisle seat with empty window seat choice. But also, there is something very beautiful about a stranger smiling at another stranger. One little moment of kindness. One small tiny glimmer of niceness in what is otherwise a quite horrendous ordeal for me.

People begin engaging with their bus activity of choice – phones, books, newspapers – productive ways to pass the time. There are a few sat simply alone with their thoughts, but I imagine they are likely still being productive. Perhaps they are going over a work presentation they have later in the day. Planning a to-do list. Planning a party. Thinking how best to tackle a tricky conversation they need to have with a work colleague.

There are endless ways to engage in productive thinking. My brain rejects them all. It simply does not have capacity for those. It will of course argue it is being productive, but I fear it may have a distorted sense of what constitutes productive.

I must focus on continually scanning and ensuring I'm aware of any potential dangers so I can protect myself. In addition to this, any dangers I have failed at protecting myself from in recent hours must be ruminated on over and over. There's a rather lot to keep my brain occupied with.

If anyone was paying attention to my appearance, which I thankfully doubt they are given how busy it is, they might likely wonder if I was in physical pain. I am perched on the front of the seat trying my hardest to ensure my body touches as little of the seat as possible. The end result is that I look like I might be suffering from some sort of back or stomach pain.

Either of these perceptions would be welcome really, given they are normal ailments, so I hope indeed they are what is concluded if anyone should decide to ponder it.

Odd as it may look, I have been instructed this is how best to keep myself safe given what I'm working with, so I have to comply.

As I near the end of the journey it's a little quieter on the bus, but I almost wish it wasn't because this could mean I am the only person departing at my stop. Departing necessitates alerting the driver to the fact that they need to stop the bus. This alert comes in the form of a bell press.

'Please someone else press the bell', 'please someone else press the bell', 'please someone else press the bell' is charmingly chanting over and over. Inside voice chanting at least – I am not the crazy lady on the bus that people avoid sitting next to. I am the crazy lady on the bus who hides it well (maybe not even well, but better than the first crazy lady).

My chanting is interrupted by the noise of the bell press. Someone has been unknowingly kind to me and pressed the bell. If they were made aware of the magnitude of their kind act, they would likely be perplexed at it being referred to as such but still, I direct to them another little silent 'thank you'.

I make my way to the door as the bus draws near to the stop, but I haven't timed it right and I'm in a standing position when the bus makes a sudden jolt.

I have two choices in this moment. I could grab onto a pole, keep upright, and avoid injury.

Or. I could listen to the screaming voice 'DO NOT TOUCH ANYTHING ON THIS BUS.' And hope and pray that balance alone will keep me upright.

Some physical instinct takes over and alerts me to the fact that if I don't touch the pole right this second, I am going to fall. Balance is not going to work. It's out. So now the choices change.

Grab onto a pole, keep upright, and avoid injury. Or. Fall onto bus floor and touch infinitely more (and worse) bus surface.

I grab onto the pole.

Thankfully I don't have to stay holding it for long as the bus soon arrives at the stop and the doors open displaying my escape.

Ok, don't panic Amy. Just do not touch any part of you (or your clothes, or your bag) with that hand until we can rectify this.

It's a cold day. I would normally have both hands in my pockets, but instead I have only one in a pocket. The other is being held slightly away from myself. As far from my side as I think I can get away with without looking weird. If that is even possible, which in this moment I try to believe it might be. I am likely deceiving myself.

I don't have far to walk to reach my office building, I feel a faint sense of relief when it comes into view. This a very minor feeling though compared to the others surging through my body.

I feel a wave of something similar to what I imagine someone might feel when a car is hurtling towards them, and they're not quite sure they have enough time to get out of its path. This sounds ridiculous doesn't it. I must be exaggerating surely.

Unfortunately, I'm not exaggerating. Not even in the slightest.

Chapter 2

I walk into my office building and an image of Ben standing outside the elevators comes into my view. Ben works in a different department to me; our paths don't cross all that often directly with work. However, we have come to know each other through the occasional social occasion and bumping into each other in the office kitchen and around the elevators.

Someone I know is always standing outside the elevators at moments like this when I don't want them to be. As if this isn't hard enough, I have to figure out some way to engage in conversation also. I don't want to chat yet. I'm not ready. I slow down my walking but he's already seen me and is clearly smiling at me so I can't really get out of this without looking rude.

I could pretend I dropped something or lost my key pass but he's the type of person who would simply come over and try and help me, thereby delaying things even further.

Ok. Try and be normal Amy.

'Morning!' 'Rubbish weather today isn't it.' 'Any plans for the weekend?' I'm not really a fan of small talk but I believe it does have its time. And this is going to be one of them – come out and shine small talk.

My ability level for conversation stops at some kind of autopilot location in these situations. It's really the best I can hope for. Ben seems happy enough to stay at this level too. I say this but I really have no idea if he's happy. I am way too distracted to take in other people's emotions right now.

We depart the elevator and I relax a tiny bit as I know I'm not far now. We are just about to part company when he turns and says, 'I think a few people are going out for drinks tonight aren't they – hope to see you there?'

He hopes to see me there. I hope to see me there too. Hoping isn't always strong enough but I stick with it and reply, 'Yes, hopefully.'

He smiles and continues on to his desk whilst I make my usual detour to the bathroom.

I feel slightly better after, but not fully. Never fully. Did I wash them enough?

I somehow manage to resist the urge to go back and instead walk in the opposite direction along to my desk.

I slept well last night – this should really translate to me arriving at work well rested, ready to be my fully charged productive self. I feel anything but rested though. I feel restless. I feel uncomfortable. I feel like I've just been through an ordeal and need time to recover.

Recovery time never arrives though, it simply doesn't seem to exist. It's always straight into the next.

That's how it operates. Any notion of resting and relief will not be entertained or tolerated.

Chapter 3

I work in an open plan office. I wish open plan offices had not become so fashionable. I understand it's an environment intended to help people feel less isolated. One big sociable, open, freely communicating group, happily all up in each other's space. No risk of anyone feeling left out or lonely in this design.

My problem is that I welcome a bit of isolation. I actively seek it out. Regularly. I prefer if at times people do not notice me. If I was hidden away in a cubicle for most of the day, I'd find this whole office thing a much easier experience.

I can't hide the crazy so well when I'm in plain visible sight of all my colleagues.

But people like me are not really considered when it comes to office design. I can concede this is fair enough. The needs of one slightly (ok, very) odd employee versus the likely majority of the rest... well, I was always going to lose. So, it gets added to my burgeoning list of things to cope with instead.

I like the people I sit next to at least. We are in a group of four desks and thankfully none of the occupants I deem too hazardous. Most of the time anyway. It can all change in a moment, but generally they do not behave in any way that alarms me on a regular basis.

Ed sits next to me and is one of my most favourite people in the world. He's kind, caring and extremely passionate about his work. This results in us talking and discussing and planning and inspiring, then realising hours have glided by. I am so thankful to him for this. He doesn't realise the extent of how amazing this time is for me, but he receives my silent gratitude every time he gifts me with this break.

Sally sits opposite me. We were a bit wary of each other at first but have come to be friends. She's very strong in her opinions and loud in her voice which is probably what put me off her on first impression.

She has endless stories to tell about how fabulous her life is and will tell them loudly to anyone who shows even a vague notion of listening. She will continue on even when people stop listening, although perhaps this is because she simply has not noticed she's lost their attention. In time though I have seen beyond this with Sally. I notice other sides of her more now, so I find myself less irritated by the loudness.

To be clear, there is irritation on both sides of the friendship – far greater really on Sally's side. She is subjected to a frequent cloud of frustration hovering over us and it has somewhat tainted our relationship.

Lastly there is Nathan who sits diagonally opposite me. Nathan is funny. Not funny weird like me. Funny that regularly induces actual streaming tears from those who hear his words. He brightens many of my days. He doesn't take life too seriously. Even at times when he really probably should. He's just in it for the laugh. I am really jealous of Nathan.

We work at a digital agency which in essence I love. It's high paced, high stress, high achieving, and high feeling. There's so much low in my life that this collection of high is much needed and addictive.

I reach my desk and am grateful to note that I'm the first one to arrive. This doesn't happen often enough for my liking. My intention is always to arrive first, but other factors often step in to prevent this intention from being fulfilled.

I take off my coat and place my bag on the floor in an exact location where I have previously assessed and deemed acceptable for it to reside. I of course still assess it again to ensure it is still acceptable.

I take out my tissues and set about making my desk a space I can feel some sort of comfort in using. Comfort is not the best word to use here really. There is no comfort in my world. I can only hope at best for some small distant resemblance of it.

The others soon arrive but thankfully I have finished before they are close enough to our desks. It doesn't always go so smoothly. I have had to become somewhat of an expert at diverting their attention whilst I carry out my necessary tasks. I say I have become an expert, but I suspect perhaps I may be deluding myself in this. No one has ever mentioned anything about it at least.

'Morning lovelies!' – this is Sally. She addresses everyone as 'lovely' but I think when it's directed at us she puts some feeling behind it.

'I know we haven't even had our morning coffees yet, so possibly too early to be thinking about alcohol, but everyone is still planning on going for drinks tonight, aren't they?'

There is a slight desperation in her voice, but it gets like that sometimes during periods of particular high stress. We've had a really busy couple of weeks, and everyone is feeling a similar need to de-stress in the pub, so we all respond without hesitation in variations of the affirmative.

I really hope I can follow through this time.

I make a quick internal plead 'Please let me.'

Chapter 4

The morning starts with a client meeting. I haven't met these clients before so it's likely going to be a bad meeting. That might sound dramatically pessimistic, but I've attended enough meetings and met enough new people to know what will happen, and then what will happen because of the thing that happened at the beginning.

My prediction is confirmed when on entering the room I am almost immediately met with an extended hand.

I've put a lot of thought into plausible reasons for why you can refuse to shake someone's hand. Plausible polite reasons that is. The best I've ever been able to come up with is that I've just applied hand cream but that oddly doesn't always deter people. However, I've used that excuse too often in front of others in this room, a few of which flat out know I have definitely not just applied hand cream.

So, I shake the hand in front of me and bid farewell to focus.

Half-way through the meeting I can feel Ed's eyes on me. My awareness spreads to the others in the room and I quickly register the silence. Oh. They're waiting for me to speak. Shit, who asked me a question and what was it? Mere seconds pass before Ed steps in and saves me by repeating the question (most likely expertly re-worded).

I answer with ease. I know my job pretty well. I have well thought-out opinions and am comfortable voicing them. Answering questions is not the problem.

When the meeting ends, I dart out the room as fast as politeness allows and head straight for the bathroom.

Later in the afternoon I'm waiting outside a room for another meeting (this time no new people so it should be lower on the stress scale). Sally is in the room talking to another colleague Lauren. They've just finished their own meeting and are gathering up their things. I am not a fan of gossip and therefore, do not go out of my way to eavesdrop on other people's conversations but given the space we are all occupying I can't help but hear their words.

It soon becomes apparent they are

discussing this evening's drinks and I hear Lauren ask Sally who is all going that she knows of. Sally reels off the list and then adds one cutting sentence to the end of the list.

'And maybe Amy. But it's unlikely really. She's a canceller.'

'Ah right. That's a shame. I like Amy.'

'I like her too but I'm not sure she likes the rest of us sometimes. She can hardly ever be bothered to make the effort to socialise with us. She'll no doubt come up with some excuse.'

She's not entirely wrong. I am a canceller.

She is wrong about the being bothered to make an effort part though. I love spending time with them and would love if I could socialise with them more. It's just not as simple for me as it is for other people.

It's immensely far beyond a straightforward choice of wanting to or not wanting to.

I don't reach the end of the day and simply decide with ease that I'd rather be at home on my own watching TV. I reach the end of the day and something else steps in and decides for me.

You're just not equipped to continue with this day Amy – home it is for you. No arguments.

I could be hurt by hearing Sally's words. I am hurt. But it would be unfair to direct my hurt at her. I can't blame her for the way she feels. She is only reacting in a natural way to the facts presented to her.

I walk back down the corridor to make sure they don't see me when they leave the room. If they saw me, they would have to ponder whether I had heard their words and there is no need for any awkwardness to be created from this.

I try not to dwell on it too much but is that even possible? It's a catalyst for other thoughts I seem powerless to hold back.

I am sure Sally is not the only one that has attached this perception to me. It feels so unfair to be viewed this way when it's not the truth. My behaviour is the truth of course, but the reasons behind my behaviour are not known by anyone so they are left with having to infer them.

Perhaps what they infer is better than the actual truth though. It is entirely possible the truth may lead them to extricate themselves from our friendship altogether, as soon as politely possible.

So, be it truth or inference, I can't win either way.

The day continues on but it's only moving in a downward direction for me.

The weight of hearing Sally's words, along with numerous little anxiety inducing incidents that occur throughout the rest of the day, all mount up to beat me down.

Not long after six o'clock people start making movements towards the pub. Sally asks, 'Anyone ready to go now? I think I'm done for the day.'

I am also done for the day. But my done does not mean the same as Sally's unfortunately. I am done with the day as a whole, needing it to be over in its entirety. Sally is simply done with the work portion.

I wish I could keep going. I wish I could go to the pub. I intended to go to the pub. I didn't lie when I told everyone previously that I was going to go. But I'm about to lie now when I reply, 'I'll meet you down there, I just need to finish some stuff first.'

They almost certainly see the lie for what it is. So, I'm treated to their usual responses.

Sally's resigned tinged with disappointment and annoyance 'Ok, see you there!'. She's long given up on challenging me every time.

Ed's simply kind 'I'll wait for you.'

Nathan's blunt but friendly 'Ames, you better definitely turn up! Do I need to wait too and drag you there myself?!'.

Those are their words but the expressions

that flit between them are painful to receive. I read them fluently. They think I don't want to spend time with them. They think I don't value our friendships. They think I can't be bothered. They think maybe I've had a better offer. They think I'm anti-social.

They'll think all these things and be disappointed and annoyed with me, but then ten minutes later I will be long forgotten from their thoughts. They will be in the pub, drinking, socialising and enjoying their evenings.

I, on the other hand, am not so lucky in the forgetting. I will go home and ruminate over how I always let down my friends. Ruminate over how I'm missing out on a fun night as I'm no longer allowed to freely participate.

One more fun occasion I have been robbed of attending. I add it to the pile of mounting evidence of how I'm failing. Failing at being alive.

In my mind, there is only one night actually ruined by my non-attendance.

It takes some time, but eventually I manage to persuade Ed not to wait for me.

'I could help with what you're working on and maybe we'd get it done faster together?'

'I don't think so. I just need to focus on it myself. Thanks though.'

'Ok. I understand. I'm still happy to hang

back and wait for you though, there's always stuff I can do here to keep myself occupied.'

'I'm sure, but there's no point us both missing out on valuable drinking time. You'll make me feel bad for holding you back.'

We continue back and forth in this vein for a little while longer before I think he senses I need him to not wait. He looks at me as if he's unsure though and can't quite decide the best thing to do.

'Honestly Ed, just go, I will see you there in a bit.'

He pauses a little longer and I make the mistake of turning to look at him. I am thrown by the look of compassion in his eyes.

Despite knowing that it's likely they are all now aware when I'm lying, I can still vaguely delude myself that they do actually believe me. As though there is nothing horrible lurking beneath the surface of our words.

His look right now is making it extremely hard to tune into that delusion and it's uncomfortable to observe so I look back to my screen.

He finally says, 'Ok, I'll leave you to it then.'

Once he has packed up his stuff and left, I lay down my pretence and let my gaze drift from my laptop. It moves to the window where it rests and contemplates the city beyond. A city so full of life. Full of people living out fun exciting experiences every single minute.

I am stuck in this moment watching. I am stuck in most moments watching.

I stay like this for a while. Tormenting myself with images of other lives. It feels cruel but I can't seem to stop.

I need to move. I need to go home and try not dwell too much on what I'm missing out on but I'm not sure that's ever going to be possible. Not today. Not any day.

Today somehow feels worse though. It feels like it's coming again. I'm slipping.

Chapter 5

I wake up the next morning and almost instantly feel confirmation that it has indeed come to visit.

I stare at the wall for a while trying to decide whether I might be able to manage. Maybe this is just a light version and I'll still be able to make it outside. Still be able to somehow trick my body into moving through a workday.

I'm just fooling myself though really. I know I can't. My head feels too fragile, I know I must handle with care.

I send my boss a message saying I'm not feeling well and won't be in. This is not a lie.

I go back to sleep.

I wake up later and do some more wall staring. Then fall back asleep again.

This is pretty much the extent of activity in my day. It's rather exhausting.

Even brain activity isn't all that high. I guess not moving all day is deemed a relatively safe predicament.

It's amazing how little a day can pass by with. I don't even register boredom. It seems this should surely have been present, at some points at least.

You would presume the volume of day sleeping would ruin my chances at night sleeping. But strangely not. The night drifts into dreamworld as usual with very little struggle.

The next day continues on in an almost identical repeat performance of the previous one. I exist in a trance like numb state flitting between staring and sleeping.

All my feelings seem to have got fed up and have fled my body. Perhaps they felt over-exerted and couldn't cope. They've left to find a more stable carrier, it's clearly way too stressful in this one.

When I travel back to dreamworld that night, I experience a really beautiful dream. Not beautiful in the sense of some magical existence with no link to reality. More so, beautiful in that it relives a time in my past. A time I have great fondness for.

I'm back in my life of about a decade ago, living a very happy life with my boyfriend at the time. It's so blissfully carefree and joyful. Our lives were glossy in their simplicity. Focus was directed solely on where the next hit of fun was coming from.

No stress. No anxiety. No peculiar alarming brain activity. No sadness.

There was probably some sadness. No life has none. But I can't remember it so it can't have been a strong force. It's absent from this dream as it was mostly absent from my life back then.

Somewhere along my reality path it transformed from being mostly absent to being mostly present.

The contrast between my then and my now is vast.

My then was a life that you would likely classify as normal. I wish I had appreciated it more. I participated. I engaged. I had fun. I worried sure, but I worried about the same things lots of other people worry about. 'Healthy' worry if it were to have a label attached. No cause for real alarm bells.

Slowly somewhere at some time though an alarm bell decided to start making some noise. It was really quiet at first, you possibly wouldn't even hear it. Was there a noise? Did you hear that? I could pretend it had been imagined since it was so faint.

Gradually over time it wasn't happy being

ignored though and realised it had to get louder. For some reason it really wanted to be part of my life so I could ignore it all I wanted, it was not going anywhere.

I hear it loud and clear these days. It's near impossible to pretend and ignore.

Chapter 6

I wake up the next morning, the dream of my life before abruptly over, and awareness of reality seeds and grows. I feel like I'm coming down off the biggest high. I don't want it to be over. I don't want this world, take me back to the other. I keep my eyes closed and stay still in a will to fall back, but it's a losing battle.

Sadness swarms and hovers over me. It slowly injects itself and tears start preparing their journey.

This dreaming pattern happens quite frequently. I cannot decide if it is cruel because it is taking me back to happier times before harshly ripping those times away from me again. Or, it may be a nice thing because for those beautiful pretend hours I have a break. I am happy and healthy.

Perhaps it is a bit of both.

Sadness appears every time on waking from these dreams but today I acknowledge this may indicate something else. It may indicate improvement. I'm not really sure whether in general it's better to feel nothing or feel something during these visits. But the pattern they follow is usually a progression from nothing to something, so I guess I'll say it's better to feel something.

I lay a while letting the tears fall, reliving the dream in my mind. Grieving my past.

I realise though that today I need to get out of bed. No, I'm still not going to make it out of the house, but I'm not allowed to stay in bed any longer. It won't let me. It doesn't sit well to give it any positive airtime, so I'll just say this quickly then move on... one good thing is that it won't allow personal hygiene to slip as that will only result in more fear.

So, I get out of bed and transport myself into the shower. I stand there for a long time simply and solely crying. I can't seem to stop. There is not much energy behind this, I'm not even sure my face is moving all that much. Tears are simply running continuously down my face.

One lone thought is on a loop in my head. 'Am I ever going to be able to properly function as a human being?'

People will sometimes advise, 'have a good cry, it'll make you feel better'. Does it though? I'm pretty sure what will make me feel better right now is not crying. Or even just feeling like I might actually be capable of stopping sometime soon.

I eventually leave the shower and get dressed. I think I'm still crying but it appears to have achieved autopilot status now so I can at least somewhat ignore it.

I go and sit in front of my laptop searching for something to distract me. I try to watch a film. Deliberately picking a light looking comedy with one of my favourite actors.

I can't concentrate on it though. Every time my favourite actor speaks, he seems to annoy me. I don't find the jokes funny. I don't understand the story. Hardly surprising given my brain can't seem to hold any of the actor's words once I've finished being annoyed with them.

I decide to read some news sites instead. Not the smartest move I know. Adding outside world negativity on top of my own is going to take me nowhere good.

I read about a horrific car crash that resulted in multiple fatalities. After the natural reactive feelings of shock and sadness for the families I turn to the less natural reaction of guilt.

I of course didn't cause the crash so not the common kind of guilt. But there's this thing called survivor's guilt where if you are involved in an accident and other people die but you survive, you feel guilty because you weren't the one that died.

You were spared for some reason, but you don't understand why so you weirdly feel guilty that the universe chose someone else to die over you. The words 'it should have been me' or 'if I'd been sitting a couple of seats over' might be uttered from your mouth.

This is a natural reaction when you live out a traumatic experience side by side with those who died. I seem to have it though when I haven't been anywhere near the experience.

I picture the people who died in my head and make an assumption that they were living great lives. They were engaging in lots of activities life has to offer, contributing well to society in their careers or hobbies, influencing friends and family with wonderful relationships. All that good stuff that you're meant to be doing.

Then I compare it to the shambles I'm being forced to make of my own life, and it seems deeply unfair. I wish desperately that I could swap with them. If there was some easy way to make this happen, I would not hesitate one single fraction of a second. They should be alive, not me.

After adding my warped version of survivor's guilt to the feelings returning to my body, I move away from the news sites.

I decide to try and eat something, but nothing tastes all that nice. I am eating similar foods to what I regularly eat but they are somehow taking on different textures today. I even try my best option for what would be deemed 'comfort food' but the comfort part seems to be missing.

It would appear that my taste buds are feeling sad too. They want to be left alone, rejecting invitations from flavour.

I give up on food and go back to searching for some other distraction.

The day continues on in a cycle of starting and abandoning activities. I feel agitated and restless. Agitation so great it feels as though it has seeped so far within it has reached my soul.

I eventually call an end to the day around early evening (ok, late afternoon) and go back to bed. I glance at my phone which has been left ignored all day. There's a message from Ed.

Hey Amy, how are you doing? Can I bring you anything? Soup? Vitamins? Tales of office gossip?

I begin a response, but my mind can't settle on the right words. It really shouldn't be this hard to reply. It's a simple friendly text message, not some instruction to provide a well thought out argument debating the current political situation. But my brain just won't form words that make any sense.

I'll reply tomorrow. I put my phone down and cocoon myself in my bed. The first vague feeling of something resembling happiness pops up when the thought crosses my mind that I might soon fall back to the previous night's dream.

Chapter 7

Day four is a repeat of day three. At least it's the weekend now so I don't have to deal with having to contact work.

Around lunchtime Ed calls me but I don't pick up. I stare at my ringing phone and will it to stop.

Early evening and he tries again. Again, I don't pick up. I just don't have words for people. Even for Ed. Maybe I have forgotten how to speak. It has been days now since I've said anything out loud.

He sends a text.

I'm a little worried. Can you just at least send a quick reply and let me know you're ok?

I'm not deliberately ignoring him in some warped attempt to gain attention or because I don't care that people worry about me. It's partly the brain not forming words thing, and partly that

I can't quite grasp that they are genuinely worried.

I convince myself that even if their worry is genuine it will only be fleeting. They will be engaged in some fun activity when they are briefly reminded that they haven't seen me in a while and perhaps that is cause for concern. They'll send a quick message but then go back to their activity and all further thoughts will be void of my existence.

Even when he has specifically spelled out his worry to me, I can't quite fathom that it's actually legitimate worry. Despite this, I sense a feeling that I should probably reply to him now. I still have the issue, however, of knowing exactly what to say.

I am in a fragile state at this moment in time and he has asked if I'm ok. I'm really not ok. I don't want to lie to him. But how can I answer truthfully without causing him further concern. I know I have to be especially careful with my words to Ed because of something that's happened in the past. Thinking of this forces me into realisation that he definitely needs a reply.

I guess these are moments when you do just lie. Lying is not always a bad thing. I just struggle to do it to Ed.

Will be back soon.

This suddenly pops into my head as a good response so it's what I send. I have not confirmed that I'm ok but neither have I lied. Hopefully it's enough.

The weekend continues on with little activity, but gradual signs of it preparing to leave are popping up quite frequently so I know I am improving.

Monday eventually arrives and I acknowledge that too many more days at home will be drifting into dangerous territory with work. They aren't going to accept the unexplained illness thing much longer. It will become a bigger deal and doctors will need to be involved in order to sign me off. Or worse.

I know I'm not in that place. I am feeling somewhat better. But I also know not to push it, it has to leave in its own time.

I let my boss know I should definitely be back tomorrow; I just think it would better to take this one more day.

They thankfully accept what I have told them with relative ease, sparing me any further distress. I am perched in instability at the moment, I have limited reserves for needing to argue and fight over this, so I am grateful when none are required.

Hopefully I can return to work tomorrow and all concerned will just treat this as a normal physical short-term illness I have suffered – some sort of virus that requires a little longer to be off sick for, but nothing anyone needs to genuinely seriously worry about.

I can usually get away with this because so far, its visits have been quite short compared to what others suffering the same experience. I know I am quite lucky in this. If luck is even the right word.

Maybe it doesn't stay very long because I'm not that great a host – a few days to a week and it's gone.

I'm still left with the other one annoyingly – that one has unfortunately become quite attached and settled. I'm not sure I can classify it as a visitor anymore since it has well and truly moved in.

Stayed beyond its welcome but it doesn't give a shit, it isn't leaving any time soon.

Chapter 8

The next day I do manage to successfully make it into work and when I arrive at the office Ben is at the elevator again.

'You missed a good night out last week; shame you couldn't make it in the end.'

'I know, I wish I could have come.' These words are not a lie at least.

'I've got a day full of meetings today – think I'm going to need a lot of coffee to get me through. In fact, I might nip over the road to get some of the good stuff before heading up. Fancy coming?'

'I would but I think I better go straight up. I've been off sick and will no doubt have a lot to catch up on.'

'Oh, sorry to hear that. You'll probably need some help getting through the day too then – I can pick you up a coffee too and drop it at your desk if you like?'

'That's so sweet, but really I'm fine.' And also, I don't drink coffee. But it seems like it might add unnecessary force to the rejection if I add in that fact, so I don't.

'Ok, well if you change your mind, I'll probably be making several trips today so feel free to join.'

We exchange smiles and he heads off back to the main door.

As I exit the elevator on my floor I bump into Nathan.

'Amy! So good to see you back. I was going to start attempting to cover your work, but you know I'm no good at the pretty pictures.'

I smile. 'No, best you keep to the curly brackets.'

He chuckles at our shorthand. Nathan is a coder and I am a designer. Neither of us really understands what the other one truly does so we reduce it to these more manageable ridiculous depictions.

'Seriously though Ames, you have been missed around here. No one to laugh at my jokes. Ed has taken on the role of Mr Grumpy. And Sal… well, she's just moaning about the work backing up, but we know deep down there's a heart somewhere and she's missed you too.'

'Thanks Nathan, I've missed you guys too.'

When I reach my desk, I see Ed is already in and his expression on seeing me is a complex mixture of happiness, concern, and relief.

'Hey, you're back.'

'I am, yes.'

'Good.' He looks at me as if debating on whether to try and talk about why I was off or whether it's better not to talk about it.

I decide to rescue him from this anguish and ask him about work. He complies and starts catching me up on everything I've missed.

It's not long before we are interrupted though as we are called into an impromptu team meeting.

Once everyone is settled in the meeting room, Sally takes the lead and starts talking about an important upcoming piece of work. She informs us that it is going to involve working very closely with our Sydney office. As a result of this, the company has decided it would be good to get everyone together for initial planning.

'So, how does everyone feel about a trip to beautiful Australia!?'

'Well… if we absolutely must force ourselves to spend a couple of weeks in the sun, surf, and beautiful scenery then I will try and not complain too much I suppose.' Nathan responds.

'Hilarious Nathan. I take it everyone agrees

it will be amazing and is happy to go?'

I do agree it will be amazing Sally. I'm just not so sure I'll be allowed to actually partake in the amazement. But I stay silent and just smile along with the collective agreement of the others.

'Ok great, I will go ahead and start investigating flights then and be in touch with the details. Go forth and buy all the necessary sun appropriate attire no doubt missing from all our wardrobes.'

There is a buzz of excitement around the office for the rest of the day. This I do at least get to partake in because I can exert a bit of pretending here. Not pretending to be excited – more so, pretending that nothing will stop me from going on the trip.

'You will go won't you?' Ed asks later when we're alone at our desks. 'I mean, I know it's a big trip and quite a trek to get there but Sydney's an amazing place, you'll love it there.'

'I really want to. I just need to think about it.'

'Don't do that. Maybe try not thinking about it? I think sometimes thinking gets you into trouble.'

He is not wrong. Not wrong at all.

I laugh my response to keep it light. 'Yes, that does sound like me doesn't it. Ok, I promise not to think.'

I shouldn't use the word promise. But I do really want to try.

Our conversation is cut short by Nathan and Sally returning from a meeting. Nathan informs us excitedly that he thinks he has just met his soul mate.

I should clarify that pretty much every female Nathan meets he predicts to be his soul mate on first encounter.

'Erm, what??' Sally reacts. 'She flat out rudely ignored you most of the meeting and the words she spoke to others were not entirely charming.'

'I think she was just taken off guard by the spark charging between us.'

'Let me guess, she was blonde, tall, with very pretty eyes.' Ed explains.

Sally laughs. 'Spot on Ed.'

'Bless you Nathan. Maybe try taking in the whole picture before assessing for soul mate status?' I suggest.

'You guys don't get it. It's about the spark! I'm going to email her, send me her details Sal.'

Sally rolls her eyes and ignores his request.

I have viewed Nathan as pretty much single the whole time I've known him. He is not short of female attention and has had lots of relationships – just very brief relationships. He gets excited about their potential to be his soul mate but then seems to lose interest pretty quickly.

Perhaps he's just good at realising when something isn't making him happy anymore and doesn't see the point in dragging it out. Where others may stick with something and give it more of a chance, he will opt instead for quickly moving on.

He simply doesn't want to waste any time being vaguely unhappy if he can do something about it. Whether that ends up being to the detriment of his soul mate search I do not know. But I do know that he has always appeared consistently happy in the time I've known him so perhaps he has something good figured out.

Chapter 9

Once Sally starts investigating potential flights, she begins talking actual dates. She starts canvasing us all for our availability.

Everyone lets her know specific dates they absolutely can't do, but I am deliberately vague and silent for most of these conversations.

I have no prior commitments that would prevent me going but I'm also struggling to commit to saying this out loud. I am more drawn instead to keeping this as a possible excuse option for not going if I need it.

I could suddenly remember a wedding of a distant cousin I had committed to attending ages ago and forgotten all about.

I'm not sure if Sally can see my angle here or it's just the fact she likes everything properly and concisely confirmed and organised, but after a few days she says to me directly, 'Amy, I've just emailed you the dates it's looking like I am going to book – can you triple check them with your diary please and email me your confirmation to say they are definitely good for you?'

I glance at the email and notice it is addressed only to me. This, along with the fact she's discussing this with me when no one else is around, makes me conclude it's fair to say she has indeed seen my angle and is going to force the matter. We are sat inches from each other so we could easily have simply spoken words of confirmation, yet she has opted for email as her chosen method of correspondence because she wants proof.

Unfortunately, she hasn't chosen her time quite wisely enough because Ed suddenly appears back at his desk and he's just in time to overhear our conversation.

He sits down and after appearing to check his email says, 'Sal, I don't seem to have got your email, can you forward it again?'

She starts to appear annoyed and answers shortly, 'I already know the dates are fine with you.'

'Right, ok great.' He answers not questioning yet what is really going on.

I completely understand why she's doing this. I do. I have pushed her into treating me this way. I know all this, but my reaction is to meet her with my own feelings of annoyance. On account of this I can't help myself but to rebel against her request and simply answer verbally instead. 'Those dates are fine with me.'

She looks at me as if wondering how to play her next move. She's not in the mood to give in so she answers, 'Great, pop that in an email back to me and I'll go ahead and book the dates.'

Ed looks up, 'Huh? She's just told you the dates are fine, yet you still want her to email you? You're taking this digital communication thing a bit far aren't you?' he says jokingly. He's still not quite worked out yet what's going on. He's still in the light confusion stage.

She looks exasperated now. She is annoyed he has got involved. 'Yes, I want her to email me her confirmation ok?'

'But you didn't ask me to do that?'

'No, I didn't. But you I can rely on.' She explains bluntly.

He gets it now.

I stay silent.

Ed sighs. 'You're being ridiculous. Amy does not need to email you. Just go and book the flights.'

'Just stay out of it Ed, it's none of your business what I ask or don't ask Amy to do.'

They are glaring at each other now. Great

Amy, now look what you're causing.

'It's fine.' I finally interject. 'I will email you Sally, don't worry.'

'No don't Amy. She's being totally out of order.'

'It's fine, just relax ok. If she wants an email so desperately, I will send her the fricking email.'

I go ahead and do just that.

It's wrong of me to direct my annoyance at Sally, I am aware. I just really can't seem to stop myself.

We are all completely silent for the next hour, bubbling in our collective cloud of annoyance, pretending to be engrossed in work.

Ed eventually breaks the silence when he turns to me and says, 'Fancy taking a long lunch break with me? Think I might go check out that new photo exhibition I was telling you about the other day.'

He sees me thinking before quickly continuing on, 'It's not too far, walking distance I promise.' He doesn't know exactly why but he knows if I can walk somewhere I am more likely to be persuaded to go.

It would be good to get away from this horrible tension. Plus, given it's lunch time, I've only endured half a day of struggle so it's easier (marginally anyway) to summon some energy to attempt something new.

'Ok sure.' I answer before allowing myself to think on it any longer.

'Great!' he beams back at me. 'Let's leave in five?'

'Sounds good.'

Chapter 10

Once we're out of the office and a little way along the street I say, 'Sorry you got dragged into all that with Sally. It was very sweet of you to try and defend me.'

'No worries. She was being totally ridiculous.'

I don't want to turn this into a being mean to Sally conversation, so I don't dwell on it any longer and instead change the subject to some work we've been doing.

We chat for a while on that before spending what is, for the most part, an enjoyable visit walking round the photo exhibition.

We discuss each piece in depth and work out what inspiration we will take from it, if any. We don't always agree on what we consider good and not so good but that's part of the joy of experiencing this with Ed. He makes me look at things differently and appreciate perceptions I had never considered before.

We are engrossed in discussion of one particular piece when a man appears at my side with two chairs. 'I'm just setting these out in a few places round the exhibition. This piece is proving quite popular and I can see you two have been here a little while so here – please do sit.'

I look down at the chairs and see they are old, worn, and covered in what I hope is paint stains, but I can't of course be sure. There is no way I can sit on one of them. His gesture to put out chairs for people is such a kind one, I know I should graciously accept. But I can't.

'Oh, thank you, that's kind but I'm fine standing.' I reply.

He seems confused by this, perhaps wondering if I'm just being polite as I think he's brought me his own personal chair or something. I'm not sure, but he continues on, 'Please, really, these seats are for visitors – do sit and enjoy the piece a little longer.' Maybe his angle is just to get people to appreciate the work for even longer.

'Really, thank you, but I'm honestly fine standing.'

He forms this almost hurt look on his face as though I have been rude in rejecting his offer. Seriously, it's just a chair, does he have to make such a big deal? I don't think I have been rude but if he continues on it won't be long before it comes out, because rudeness unfortunately always wins over sitting somewhere I don't want to sit.

Thankfully Ed steps in before the crazy has time to take over and says, 'Thanks mate, we're actually just moving on, so we'll leave these for the next people.'

He guides me away and tries to make light of it by saying to me, 'Wow, he really took his chair distributing job seriously didn't he.'

I smile but I don't feel any happiness behind it. I try to tell myself this isn't a big deal. There are lots of reasons why people don't want to sit in chairs. The issue in my head is bigger though. Here is a person who had gone to the trouble of showing me a kind act and I had to reject it.

This is far from an isolated incident. Granted they don't all involve chairs, but I am often in situations where I have to reject kindness because the kind act becomes twisted in my head to translate to something inducing alarm. Very far from the intended niceness.

This makes me incredibly sad because people don't understand. Why would anyone reject a kind act? It makes no sense to them. So, they can only assume I must be rude. I must be ungracious and unappreciative.

I am none of those things. I am simply scared. So. Very. Scared. All. The. Time.

Ed interrupts my thoughts by asking me what I think about the new piece I realise we're currently standing in front of. Somehow, he successfully draws me into conversation about it and we continue on having an enjoyable visit.

Aside from the little chair blip leading to familiar sadness filled thinking, the visit really has been enjoyable.

The time passes so quickly I am disappointed when he says, 'We should really head back now. There's taking a long lunch and then there's just plain taking the piss.'

I smile. 'Guess so. Ok, let's walk back. Thanks for this though, you've brightened what started out as a pretty miserable day.'

He smiles back. 'Good to hear. It's brightened my day too.'

Chapter 11

A couple of evenings later we are all working late to meet a deadline the following day. There is nothing strictly for Sally to do but she stays on anyway. She always does when others in her team need to work late. She is not obliged to do this at all, it is certainly not part of her official job description as project manager. She will argue it is part of her job description though, simply falling under the realm of looking after her team.

She will do coffee runs, she will order us dinner, she will go to the shops if anyone feels like they need something. Any way possible that presents itself for her to help she will happily do so.

She doesn't hover or do all this in a disruptive way. For someone who has a default setting of loud and chatty, she somehow manages to curtail this and generally only speaks when she knows it will be of some genuine help.

It's all very lovely of her.

Nathan and Ed decide to go for a walk to the coffee shop themselves at one point as they feel the need for a break.

'I think we're not actually that far off finishing now so it shouldn't be crazy late tonight.' I let her know.

'Great. Do you have five minutes for a quick break and chat then?'

'Sure. What's up?'

'Remember the woman we were talking about the other day who Nathan decided to fall in love with?'

'Hmm... remind me, which one?'

She smiles, 'The one that was here for a meeting and was really rude to everyone.'

'Oh yes. What about her?'

'She emailed me earlier asking for Nathan's details. She asked under the flimsy pretence of needing to send him something. So, I replied saying she could just send whatever to me and I would forward it on. Her response was that she felt it would build a better relationship with us if everyone on the team was contactable.'

'Well, some clients are like that so it's not entirely implausible that she would say that I guess.'

'No. Not entirely. But I just get the feeling that was not her angle.'

'Didn't you say she ignored him in the meeting though?'

'She did pretty much. But maybe Nathan was right. People do seem to fall in love with him as much as he falls in love with others. But regardless of how she feels I don't really want to encourage a relationship. Nathan hasn't asked me again for her details so I was hoping it wouldn't go any further.'

'You're sweet to want to protect him but maybe this woman is not so bad. She might have just been having an off day when you met her? Maybe she'd just spilt coffee on her new expensive outfit, or she'd heard there were redundancies being made in her company, or some other kind of bad news. Loads of possible reasons. I know it doesn't excuse her rudeness, but we all have moments when we are not our best. She might actually be a really lovely person.'

'Or, she might just be like that all the time and Nathan will fall in love with her regardless and we will be subjected to her at all future social occasions.'

I smile. 'I think you should pass on the details and let them figure it out.'

'I'm wishing I hadn't asked you now, I knew you would give me an answer I wouldn't want.' she smiles.

'If it makes you feel better, I would guess you will still likely get your preferred outcome in the end anyway. If she is genuinely interested, they'll go on a few dates, he'll get bored and it will naturally fizzle out.'

'True.'

Sally genuinely cares for Nathan, and wants him to be happy, of that I have no doubt. However, I suspect her frequent meddling in his love life is given strength more so by the fact he gives her more attention when he's single.

Chapter 12

The following weeks pass in a whirl of planning and organising. I take on an almost separate existence. An existence of someone who is in no doubt about going on this trip.

I respond to all Sally's questions and requests such as what is required information needed for travel arrangements.

I go shopping for new things I might need for the trip. Miniature toiletries, summer clothes, sunglasses. All the normal things one might purchase for a trip abroad.

Plus a few non-normal things.

Bottles of handwash just in case they don't have any in the hotel. Even if they do have some, it would be unlikely I'd be comfortable using them.

New towels that I will use only on this trip then dispose of them on return. If it was possible to fit bedding in my suitcase I would take my own of that too, but as I am confined by space I concede this is something I will just have to try and cope with.

Packets of tissues. Numerous packets. I'm sure I will be able to buy some once there, but I have to make sure I have enough for the journey and until I am within distance of a shop.

I move my body through each day as best I can under the pretence of someone excited about going on holiday.

I engage in the planning conversations with enthusiasm. Somewhat tainted, Amy level enthusiasm that is. It is always prevented from reaching its full potential as anxiety will step in to ensure this never happens. But I can feign something resembling it at least at times.

Ed has lots of suggestions for things for us to do. He spent some time living in Sydney, so we are all happy to defer to his opinions and ideas.

Bars, restaurants and cafes feature highly in his suggestions. I know he was really into water sports when he lived there but he doesn't give these too much spotlight in his ideas. I know he's doing this for my benefit.

He of course doesn't leave them out completely as he wants everyone to have a good time and a good experience, but he is careful with his words to ensure there is no pressure to participate. And neither will he make anyone (ok, mostly me) feel like they are really missing out if they don't want to do something.

As the trip draws nearer, I try to absorb myself in work. I'm changing tact now. Keep your mind busy with work Amy and pretend the trip does not even exist. If it doesn't exist there is no cause for concern. No need to alert anxiety to the fact its presence is required.

Chapter 13

When our departure day eventually arrives, Ed picks me up on the way to the airport. It's not on his way but I suspect this is his way of gently ensuring I do actually turn up. Good strategy Ed.

I really have been back and forth quite a bit about whether to go on this trip or not. It would have been something I'd be so excited about doing before. I would have looked forward to it for weeks, focused solely on all the opportunities for fun and new adventure.

My focus has wobbled quite substantially in my current reality. All the opportunities for potential discomfort have made an unwelcome prominence, well and truly dulling the shine off any excitement.

I used to love travel so much. I loved it even more if it involved going on a plane. I loved the sensation of being high up in the sky sitting next to the clouds. This love has been somewhat surpassed by other feelings now. It has been all but abandoned, replaced by fear.

Not fear of flying in the way other people fear it. I have no fear of bad turbulence, or the far greater worry of being subjected to a plane crash. I have fear of being subjected to merely sitting in a plane with no control over my surroundings.

All the things I fear on a short bus journey are elevated to a dizzily high new level on a plane. If I start to feel anxiety I cannot simply get off at the next stop and extricate myself from the discomfort with speed.

I am well and truly trapped.

So, the idea of being on even a short haul flight will present to me not an overly appealing prospect. London to Australia is one of the longest flight journeys I think that exists so why am I even vaguely contemplating it?

This feels like too big a challenge. Too big a challenge to attempt. But also, too big a challenge to not attempt.

I've gradually watched event after event evade my presence. I've tried to ignore the fact and pretend they were not too big a deal and I would simply attend the next one. But more and more of the next ones have fallen down the same drain of avoidance.

Some have affected me more than others

and as the days passed in the lead up to the Australia trip I have become more and more aware of a strong wave of feeling I can't quite identify. It feels like it's trying to warn me. It's trying to warn me the importance of this trip. If I don't go this might be the one to damage me beyond repair.

I try to apply some logic to my decision and think through possible outcomes.

If I do go, I might spend a large amount of time in a state of distress. But then, that is pretty much my default setting at home too. I might have some kind of breakdown in front of my work colleagues, causing them to harshly judge me and realise I'm weirder than they already suspected. They might distance themselves from me and I might end up losing them as friends. I might have to leave my job as it's too uncomfortable being that person people have the story about from Australia.

If I don't go, however, it will be like accepting the big seal of confirmation that hovers over my head. 'This thing is ruining your life Amy' confirmation. Then the other thing will come and visit. The thing that engulfs me in sadness. It might stay longer this time. Maybe it would never leave.

I have repetitively gone back and forth assessing which has the risk of the worse outcome and I realised that the outcome of one choice is almost certainly guaranteed, whereas the other does have some potential for good.

There is a small (slightly delusional I can concede) part of me that wonders if perhaps leaving my life here could end up being some kind of miracle cure. As though travelling through a time zone might be all I need to reset my brain and transport me back to normality.

Putting myself through a test of this magnitude might be just what my brain needs. It feels like it's worth a try even if I am potentially deluding myself.

On account of this I finally arrive at my decision when I hear Ed ringing the doorbell.

Ok, going.

Let's try Amy. Let's at least try.

Ed looks a little surprised when I open the door and he registers my appearance to match one of someone who is about to go on holiday. It's only a fleeting look though before it is surpassed by a beaming smile.

I smile back at him and I know our silent transmissions are so much more than simple excitement about going on a trip.

We're both happy I've decided to attempt this.

Ed offers to carry my suitcase out to the car and after pausing to assess, I conclude my case is going to be touched by many strangers on the journey so I may as well also let Ed.

His excited mood on the car ride to the airport is infectious and helps convince me that I made the right decision. Hanging out with my friends is fun when I get to acknowledge it, so I need to keep that momentum going and lessen the momentum of acknowledging the other.

I just hope, pray, and beg that is a possible thing to do.

'This is going to be so much fun!' Ed grins.

Believe this sentence Amy. Please believe it. Absorb it, focus on it often and hope beyond all hope that it can come true for you.

Chapter 14

Airports and I are not the best of friends. There's too much going on for me, I don't always have enough time to scan and assess. I feel control begin its departure from my grasp almost as soon as I walk in the main entrance.

When I was a kid, I loved airports. A building full of stories. The ultimate place to people-watch.

Tears streaming in response to goodbyes. Tears streaming in response to hellos. Solo travellers wishing to escape. Escape what? Families screaming at each other. They need this holiday. Business travellers about to make a career defining presentation. Or just another mundane soul-destroying commute. People leaving to start new lives in a different county, hoping they've made the right decision. People returning from living in a different county, hoping they've made the right decision.

People-watching and pondering their stories isn't something I can really expect to engage in anymore. There's no room. My focus and concentration are forced elsewhere.

Once everyone in our group has arrived, we make our way towards security. This is the first major hurdle for me. The others are all excitedly chatting away, likely giving barely any thought to what they are about to do. To them, passing through security is just a part of the airport experience. I doubt it would be described as enjoyable by anyone, but far from particularly horrendous either.

I wish I had an even vaguely similar stance to this. I am unfortunately, however, firmly in the horrendous viewing realm.

I grow quieter and quieter as the queue progresses. I need to concentrate.

On reaching the front I lift a requisite tray and, as quickly as my brain allows, form my possessions inside it ensuring the least possible contact with the tray itself.

The security man does not agree with my little formation, however, and starts squishing everything into all corners of the tray. His hands all over, touching everything.

Heat starts punching through my body.

Please stop.

Please stop Mr security man. I know and appreciate this is you trying to do your job efficiently, but this is also you freaking me the hell out.

Please stop.

I can't voice these words of course. And neither can I plead with my eyes, since he might misconstrue this as me trying to hide something. So, I look away and try and focus on walking through the security machine instead.

On the other side I desperately will my belongings to move faster down the conveyer belt thing but just as they approach reachable distance a hand rests on my arm. 'Could you step over here please.'

Can I? Yes. Only just, but yes. Do I want to? With every feeling in my body, absolutely not.

'If you could please raise your arms, I'm just going to do a quick body search.'

I imagine my level of distress at this point is somewhere similar to that of a person who is actually concealing a vast quantity of illegal substances on their body.

I am of course thankful security is taken so seriously at airports and all the searching activities are carried out. Any actions taken by others to promote fear reduction are viewed highly in my mind. But still, when it's me being subjected to the search I want to scream.

Not just in the way people say they want to scream but it's a mere throwaway comment referring only to the impact of the sentiment. In this instance, I very much literally want to scream. I can feel the loud notes rushing up through my vocal cords desperately attempting to break free.

'Get off me with your hands!' 'Please DO NOT touch me!!'

These words I cannot allow to meet air, however, or I will likely be led away to a scary room and not allowed any further on this trip. Or indeed any future trips involving air travel.

So, all the strength I am in possession of is directed at keeping them suppressed. I try and will myself to focus on breathing. Breathing will get you through this Amy. Slow deep breathes.

Just. Keep. Breathing.

When it's finally over I grab my possessions and join the others waiting for me as quickly as I can. Moving at speed cannot fix what has just happened but I still sense the need to run away from danger, so I comply.

Sometimes I feel like just running. Running fast and never stopping. Maybe I could go so far, I could outrun it. Outrun the fear and eventually reach some utopian location where there is only calm.

Another little delusional dream.

'Trying to smuggle something dodgy are you Ames? Glad I didn't decide to ask you to be in charge of my contraband.' Nathan jokes.

I half-heartedly manage a smile that is far from genuine and keep walking.

Our departure gate has not yet been revealed so people make various decisions on how to occupy themselves until then and split up.

I'm not sure what to do. I strongly feel like I need to do something to fix what's just happened. How can I undo all the hands all over me and my possessions? The only real way to rectify it would be to shower and wash my clothes but that just isn't an option here. I scramble to find some adequate alternative but I'm struggling to think of anything that will even remotely suffice.

I become aware that I really don't feel right. The fear is seeping through me. Heat is rising and swarming around all my limbs. Am I breathing right? I'm not sure. Do I even still know how to breathe? Surely you cannot forget this most basic human action but in this moment it seems like I might have.

'Amy.'

Everything is blurred out around me, my body and my fear have such heightened focus, there is none left for anything else.

'Amy?'

I can hear a sound but it's also a bit blurred. Shit. I need to fix this. Right now.

'Amy?'

Ed's hand hovers over my arm but he seems to think better of it and pulls it back. Instead he repeats my name a little louder and sharper and moves his face in front of mine.

It's enough to pull my attention and he looks at me, eyes filled with compassion, and asks quietly 'What can I do?'

What can he do. I wish there was something. I wish I could tell him all this going on inside my head. But it's so hard to explain and even if I could, he would certainly think I was crazy. His kind compassionate face would form an expression of distance and confusion as he realised there was something he really didn't understand in his friend.

I don't want to see that expression. Not from anyone, but most definitely not from Ed.

'Um, what? Nothing, I'm fine. Really. Just... think um... I'm going to go to the bathroom.' Somehow, I get these jumbled words out.

I can't be around people right now. Not people I know anyway. There is no choice to escape people altogether given I am trapped in an airport. But there is a choice to escape people I know so

I will take it. I will take any kind of choice I can because I need to claw at some control.

I manage to get myself to the nearest facilities and thankfully they are relatively empty. I stand at the wash basin and wash my hands several times but it's not enough.

It never feels enough.

The fear is still prickling at my skin.

I so desperately want to have a shower. I so desperately want to wash my clothes. Those aren't options so my hands will pay the price.

I need to move away from the basin. I need to stop. I should stop. This is silly. I just can't seem to extricate myself from this repetition. It feels like some kind of magnet I'm attached to.

Ok. Time for some strong words. Fight back Amy.

I need to make a decision about what I do next. Once I know that I will be more able to move.

After some thought I conclude I have two options.

I can leave the bathroom, leave the airport altogether, and go home. Feign some fabricated illness that will almost certainly not be believed by anyone, but do I even care at this point. They already consider me a liar and canceller. They would not be gaining any new knowledge about me so maybe wouldn't even care all that much as I had just played into their expectance.

Or, option two. I could not give in to it. This one time, I could not let it win. I could not engage with it. I could consider instead the fact that millions of other people have had a similar experience to me with being searched and they are not assigning it any cause for alarm. They are still going ahead with their travel. I should therefore be absolutely fine to get on the plane. Shouldn't I?

This isn't one of those times where the avoidance option is too easy to resist. I desperately want to go to Australia. I do not want to avoid.

Ok. Breathe.

'I am completely fine, I can do this'.

Breathe again.

'I am completely fine, I can do this'.

After repeating this several times over I glimpse sight of a little calm.

Try for option two Amy. You've got this far. Don't let this one uncomfortable experience ruin the whole trip. Keep reminding yourself of all those other travellers who are searched and they don't let it give them any grounds for reassessing their trip. Please try and stop being so ridiculous. You will be absolutely fine.

Breathe again.

I eventually manage to move away from

the basin and move myself back into the airport. I've decided on option two for now, but I know the decision is precarious. Perhaps I need it to be. Knowing I always have an out provides some small feeling of control I guess.

I hope I can stay on track but there is never any guarantee even once decisions are made. Decisions are very easily unmade in my world.

Being back with the others might help. I will them to distract me. Distraction is likely my best and only route to the plane, so let's hope my friends comply.

As I start walking back in their direction, I see Ed standing waiting for me.

He looks at me and I can see the words he's about to say but thankfully he seems to sense he shouldn't say them aloud.

I smile at him. The best smile I can summon that will transmit to him my silent answer to his silent question. Yes, I'm ok. But I won't be if you ask me. So, don't. Absolutely no asking if I'm ok. Ok?

He somehow hears these words and smiles back at me. He says out loud, 'Thought maybe we could go for a wander? Probably good to get in as much walking as we can before all the hours of sitting.'

'Sure, good idea.'

Chapter 15

As we walk Ed tells me about his time living in Sydney.

'What was it like living there?' I ask him.

'Really great. It was never my original plan to live there, I'd been travelling round nearby countries and a couple of people I met were going to Sydney and persuaded me to join them. I only planned to stay for a few weeks but once I got to Sydney, I found it hard to want to leave. So, I looked into getting a work visa and stayed on.'

'Did you know anyone there?'

'Not one person. The people I'd travelled there with stuck to their plan of only staying a couple of weeks, but I met others pretty easily.'

'That doesn't surprise me, you make friends wherever you go.'

'True. I am very likeable, aren't I?' he smiles.

'You are yes.' I smile back.

'I got a flatshare with a few other people so that's always a good way to meet people. And I got really into water sports so met people that way. I knew it was up to me though, you sort of have to get into 'yes mode'.'

'Yes mode?'

'Saying yes to everything.'

'Ah.' A notion entirely forbidden in my world.

'Sounds a bit self-helpy I know, but it does work. I mean, not everything you say yes to will be great. For example, you may find yourself at some dodgy party with strange people dressed up in unidentifiable slightly alarming costumes... but for the most part you will likely end up having lots of fun experiences.'

I smile. 'Tempted as I am to ask, I think maybe I don't want to know about the costumes, so I'll just let that hang there.'

'Yeh, probably best.' He smiles.

'So, if you were having such a great time, how come you moved back?'

'I missed home, I guess. It's hard being so far away, not being able to just pop round to your parents' house if they need you. Missing out on loads of events like weddings and birthdays. Someone gets sick and you can't reach them for days. My brother had a kid when I was there, and I realised I didn't want to miss out on being an uncle. It all just started to get to me, so I came back.'

'Do you miss it?'

'All the time. Especially in the winter. I find myself going into hibernation mode here in the winter, but over there I was going surfing after work in the evenings and all sorts of other stuff. People are just so much more up for doing stuff when the weather is good.'

I wish the weather was the only thing ever causing me to enter hibernation mode.

'But you have to compromise wherever you live don't you.' He continues, 'So, if I have to put up with rubbish weather but get to be near my family then I will still be happy.'

'Good attitude.'

'Yep. Remind me of this conversation please when I am no doubt going to be repeating 'why the hell did I leave this place?' over and over once we get there.'

'Ok, noted.' I smile.

We eventually re-join the others and tune into Nathan recounting a familiar themed story about meeting a woman in an airport once who he was sure was definitely this time his soul mate.

'I spent two hours exchanging childhood

histories whilst simultaneously planning my future with her in my head. Then she suddenly excitedly got up saying 'there they are!' whilst leaping into the arms of her husband and kids.'

He continues on, injecting the story with his usual humour.

Distraction is proving successful. Thank you friends.

Chapter 16

The plane eventually boards, and I am beyond grateful I have actually managed to make it on. One little win. Well done Amy.

The airport searching incident has added to the unsettling feeling that continually lurks in the back of my head. The feeling where you know something is wrong even when you are not specifically thinking about it. Despite this feeling being a pretty much constant in my existence, I'm not sure that equates to it being something you can eventually get used to. So, I have to just somehow accept its presence and live with it.

It will accompany me on this flight as it accompanies me through all my waking hours, but thankfully it didn't stop me boarding.

Long haul flights are somewhat surreal experiences at times. They can have strange effects on even the sanest of people. You are essentially trapped in a claustrophobic vehicle, unpredictable in its stability and offering very little in the way of personal space. You are trapped here for a period of time that will pass in a likely disproportionate speed to its actuality.

You will be told when you can sleep, when you can eat, when you must stay seated, when you can use the bathroom. You hand over a lot of control of your life when you board.

When it's the designated night-time and lights are turned off, everyone covered in blankets, it takes on a feeling of being in a mass (supremely uncomfortable, oddly shaped) bed. The only environment where you can wake up mere inches away from a stranger's sleeping face and it's socially acceptable to do so.

Thankfully on this flight I am not sleeping next to a stranger. I am sat next to Ed with Sally on the other side across the aisle. Knowing my neighbours eases one part of this environment for me at least.

It's hard though to get my brain away from the fact I'm trapped inside this thing with not a whole lot of personal space. Yes, I am aware I need more personal space than the average person, but I think most would gladly accept a little more on a plane if it were offered to them.

This is one environment where I don't have the option available to me to run. Instead I am left only with having to face everything that presents itself to me. This swings back and forth between being a good thing (of sorts) and being a bad thing.

It's a good thing because my brain seems to take on a temporary view of my body. Well, we can't do anything about this so just accept all we'd normally stop and protect you from and we'll store it all up for a major debriefing meltdown later when you're off this thing. Then I am oddly relaxed for this temporary period, as though I am inhabiting someone else's body so no damage can be done to my own.

Or, it can go the other way. Anxiety seeps into every pore of my body and I stay still, completely rigid, any modicum of comfort that may have existed now harshly eradicated. Manically searching for some form of control over my environment. I can somewhat impressively maintain a heightened state of fear for quite the length of time.

Thankfully my brain seems to be favouring the first approach for most of this flight. I will of course likely pay for it later but at least for now I can portray some normality.

The flight passes with a mix of film/ TV watching, eating, sleeping, water intake monitoring, and people complaining about cramps and/or loss of feeling in feet and/or legs.

Sally is desperate to ensure we do not forget the importance of water. She assures us that we will all suffer terrible consequences with our health if we do not drink enough of the stuff.

Despite her annoying reiteration of the advice, I do know it to be sensible and true, but I just can't really conform. If I drink lots of water the result will be needing to go more often to the toilet.

I struggle with public toilets in general, but public toilets on a plane... they are sort of the ultimate in toilet stress. Cramped, tiny, and not in any way pleasant spaces to be in for anyone, but for me it cranks up a notch. It's hard not to touch anything in there on account of space size and turbulence factors. So, there will be a lot of hand washing and working out how to get out without coming into contact with anything further.

I have heard it's incredibly bad to 'hold it in' and not relieve your bladder regularly but I'm hoping my body will take pity on me and let me off this one time. So, I barely drink anything but make a show of pretend drinking every time Sally glances my way. I also get up and wander in the toilet direction every so often so no one will realise and comment on my lack of toilet trips.

I've come to be pretty good at the pretending skill for many aspects of life. It's kind of a necessity if I want to avoid making the weird attract the spotlight.

Sally and I chat about books for a while

and are amazed to discover we've been reading the same one at (almost) the same time. I finished it a month before she started it, but for us this still constitutes as a coincidence to marvel at and we pass a not insubstantial amount of time discussing it.

We have very similar taste in books, so she is my person for recommendations. My Kindle would be severely missing out without her input. And I would be severely missing out without books. I am almost granted a proper break with them.

My brain appears seemingly tricked into being absorbed in the imaginary world of characters. It doesn't often stay tricked for long though sadly. More often than not it will abruptly realise what's happening and interject the story with – hold on, remember you are meant to be worrying about that thing that happened earlier? Come on, we need to think some more on that... So, attention won't always last or hold but it can occasionally be successful for short periods of time.

The lights are dimmed, and we soon realise we're the only ones talking in the vicinity since it is now the appointed sleep time. We know it's bad etiquette to keep talking so we agree to try and get some sleep ourselves.

Sally gets up for a toilet trip before

settling. Nathan and Ed are already asleep so that thankfully leaves me alone to carry out some very important assessing.

Here goes.

Now, in order to sleep my head is going to have to touch something. I'm not sure it's even a possible thing to sleep without your head touching anything. Maybe with your head slouched forward but it likely won't stay that way for the duration of the sleep. And it will almost certainly result in severe neck pain upon waking.

So, I'm going to have to rest my head against the back of the chair. I could put my jumper in between my head and the chair to use as a buffer but then I would be cold. I certainly can't use the provided blanket to keep me warm, so the jumper has to stay on. I really hate being cold and it would keep me awake therefore defeating the purpose of leaning back anyway.

Why did I not think to bring some kind of makeshift pillow? I start to get angry with myself for not realising this beforehand and being prepared. It seems like such an obvious necessity for someone like me now I think about it, yet, it didn't even enter my head when I was packing. I continue to curse myself despite realising this is a pointless endeavour since there is absolutely nothing I can change about it now.

Still, I can't seem to stop the annoyance. It

is almost as though I am in some state of delusion, believing there is one high up level of annoyance that if I reach, I will be popped back in time to correct my error.

Focus Amy.

The only option I am left with is to allow my head to touch the chair. I look around and observe the passengers around me. Every single one is asleep with their head touching the chair. This means I should be fine to do it too. It's normal behaviour so just be fricking normal for once Amy.

Sally has returned and fallen asleep in the time it takes me to work up the courage to put my head back and close my eyes. Even then, it's a further ten minutes of my head just sort of gently grazing the surface before I let it rest fully.

Think nice thoughts. Think nice thoughts. Don't think about the chair. Think nice thoughts. Don't think about the chair. Think nice thoughts. Think nice thoughts.

I eventually drift off into a disruptive sleep. Did I make the right decision? Should I have just stayed awake and kept my head protected away from any contact with the chair? I can't change it now, but I start up again with the deluded thinking of annoyance resulting in going back in time allowing me to change things.

Just accept it Amy. Accept it and shut up and go to sleep. I manage to act on this instruction at some point and do manage to achieve some sleep thankfully, but it's far from comfortable.

When I wake up, Ed's sleeping face is the first thing I see. He looks so peaceful. I hope he's having a nice dream. I turn away because I realise if he were to wake up at this precise moment, he would wake to see me staring at him. Whilst we are very comfortable around each other (in as much as I can be comfortable around people) this still feels like it would be a step into awkward.

Nathan appears by my side in the aisle.

'Sleep well?' he asks.

Not in the slightest. 'Not massively. I'm not even sure I was asleep very long – what time is it? Or actually, more helpful question – how many more hours to go?'

'We're not far now. I can't seem to stop myself obsessively checking the flight map. I'm pretty sure it's lying to me a lot of the time but it's currently informing that we only have another hour or so left until Singapore.'

'Oh great, that's not so bad then. It will be so nice to breathe fresh air again.'

'Yep. Although we best not get too used to it. Remind me again why we are not at least staying the night in Singapore? I'm not sure I'm built for this hard-core travelling with all the flights joined up stupidly close to each other.'

I smile. 'I know, it's not ideal but at least it gets it all over with quicker I guess.' And gives me less time to contemplate replacing the connecting flight with a return flight, I silently add.

Chapter 17

We land in Singapore for our part way stop – a mere two-hour break but everyone is still very grateful for any length of time at all away from the plane.

On entering the airport, as we are all adjusting to non-recycled air and the ability to walk further than a few steps, Nathan asks, 'What does everyone fancy doing?'

Sally and I reply in unison 'Toilet first!'. Me because I'm desperate to empty my bladder, given I only managed to face the grand total of one toilet trip on the entire fourteen-hour flight. (I know, sincere apologies bladder). Sally because she just wants space to freshen up.

We agree on a place to catch up with them and head off towards the facilities. Please be nice ones. Please be nice ones. Please be nice ones.

'I heard they have showers here; I might

investigate if that's true and we can use them.' Sally says.

'I don't think I'll bother but I'm happy to wait for you while you do.' I would seriously love a shower right now. Just not one that lives in an airport and is used by numerous strangers.

The facilities are nice thankfully. They even have those touch-sensor wash basins, so I am spared the stress of having to touch taps.

We find out that there are indeed showers albeit ones you have to pay for. It's not overly expensive though and given how nice it is to feel clean and fresh after such a long flight I think it would be money well spent.

Sally is happy to spend this money. I of course am not. It is not the monetary cost that is deterring me, it is the cost I would be charged by my brain.

There is a very nice clean spacious changing area anyway, so I sit there and wait for Sally.

'That was amazing, I feel so much better now!' she informs me once she's finished. 'Are you sure you don't want to have one?'

She looks at me with a look mixed with a little confusion and a little concern. 'We still have a long way to go.' She adds.

'Is that your polite way of telling me I smell?' I smile at her.

She laughs, 'No, of course not. I just know how long-haul travel can make people feel rubbish and so looking after ourselves, in any little way that might present itself, is worth doing in my book.'

'I know but I'm fine really. I'll just embrace the feeling rubbish I think.'

This appears to be a common activity in my life.

'Ok, suit yourself. Let's go join the others then.'

We wander back out into the airport and it's not long before we catch sight of them. It's Nathan we encounter first. He hands Sally a paper bag and says, 'I bought you a gift Sal.'

'Oh, how sweet of you!' she replies as she opens the bag and lifts out an object that I'm not entirely sure how to identify. It's a rather large, heavy looking mushroom ornament type thing. 'Erm… thanks?'

'I know you like mushrooms so I thought it would be the perfect gift for you!'

'I like mushrooms?'

'Yeh, you told me, remember that time we were all working late and we ordered the pizzas?'

Sally appears none the wiser and looks at me confused.

'Think we might need a bit more detail on this one Nathan.' I suggest.

'You requested we order a pizza with mushrooms on it.'

'No I didn't. I mean, yes, I'm sure I probably ate some pizza with mushrooms on it that someone else had ordered but it wasn't my specific request.'

'Oh, I was sure you had requested it.'

'No. Not me. But wait, even if I had Nathan - how the hell do you make the leap from liking eating mushrooms on a pizza to liking giant mushroom paperweight doorstop things?!'

I can't help but start to giggle.

'Well, um… yes… this does appear to me now to have been an odd decision I have made.'

Sally joins me with the giggles and thankfully Nathan takes no offense and joins us too.

He adds somewhat perplexed, 'Why was I thinking now was the right time to buy you this anyway even if you did like mushroom paraphernalia? You would have to lug it round for the rest of the trip and it has already made my arm sore from the short time I was holding it.'

We can't seem to stop laughing. It is disproportionate laughing to the situation, but lack of proper sleep mixed with time zone travel is clearly making us all a bit delirious.

Ed joins us and we repeat the story to him. He simply turns to Nathan and says 'Good to know. For the record, I like expensive photography equipment on my pizzas.'

'Yeh, yeh, very funny. In my defence, travel really messes me up ok? Maybe someone supervise all my purchases from now on please.'

We eventually manage to compose ourselves and go for a much needed walk around the airport. It feels so nice to walk and stretch.

After some time we are drawn to the expansive airport windows highlighting a most spectacular view. The sky is showing many beautiful colours and patterns in a seemingly photoshopped depiction. It is stunning to observe so we do just that for quite a while. The others begin talking about planes and other stuff that I tune out from. I just want this moment with the sky.

I don't quite know what it is about the sky, but it transfixes, calms and makes me smile. Maybe it's the sheer expanse of open space. I think it might represent some sort of freedom in my mind. Even on grey stormy days I wouldn't abandon it. I think it makes me love it even more. We all struggle, even the sky, but beauty never leaves us if we're open to noticing it.

I believe this to be true, yet I still struggle

often with reminding myself of it.

I stand still simply staring at the sky, letting my vision take in as much detail as I can. I feel my whole body relax. A wave of something I can't quite describe is washing through me. Right in this very moment I'm ok. I know I won't be ok again soon but right now I'm with the sky and it's letting me know it's got me.

'Amy, that's us, we need to go.' Ed says.

The words break my vision and I realise everyone else has moved away towards the boarding gate.

'Oh right, sorry.'

'Where were you?'

'Where was I?'

'Yeh, you looked miles away.'

I smile. 'Somewhere beautiful.'

He beams a smile at me. 'Nice. Sorry to tear you away then. If it's any consolation where we are heading is pretty beautiful too.'

'So I have heard. I am beginning to wonder if this one person I've been speaking to perhaps has shares in Sydney tourism…'

He laughs, 'I've been going on about it too much haven't I. I guess I just wanted to big it up to make sure you realised what you'd be missing out on if you decided not to go. But it is genuinely

THE EXISTENCE OF AMY

beautiful I have not been lying to you.'

'I'm sure it is. I think your plan worked anyway as I would be really disappointed now if I didn't get to see it.'

'Just as well you made a good decision then.'

We smile at each other and join the others at the boarding gate.

The jury is still out as to whether I did actually make a good decision in coming on this trip. Appreciating Sydney's beauty I'm sure will contribute some good, but there are so many other factors with high potential to sway it more to favour the bad.

I make a mental note to hold onto the image of the sky. I need to carry it back onto the plane with me and visually repeat it frequently to use as defence.

Chapter 18

The second flight is pretty much a repeat of the first one's activities even down to the regular water intake updates and complaining about uncomfortable body parts. This one, however, invites the feeling of apprehension to appear.

I sense it creeping up on me when we have around an hour left of the flight. Up until that point I could just pretend all I had to think about was being on this plane. Nothing next.

But as the landing time draws near it's harder to ignore the next.

I know the most sensible approach to successfully making it through this trip is to consider only the day in front of me as it comes into existence. It's hard, however, not to lump all the days together and assess them in their entirety.

Two whole weeks in an unfamiliar environment with unfamiliar people with unfamiliar and unknown activities. The only familiar thing I can guarantee to rely on is feeling anxiety. A disturbing thought.

'You doing ok?' Ed interrupts my thoughts.

'Yeh, just thinking.'

'Remember what we discussed about that?'

I smile. 'I know, it just seems pretty impossible to stop most of the time.'

'Well, I'm glad you didn't let it stop you coming. Once we get there and you see how amazing Sydney is, you'll be really happy. It'll be easier to realise you made the right choice. Sorry, I'm doing it again aren't I. I can't seem to stop myself with the amazing Sydney stuff, but I guess I am feeling the need to keep reminding you.'

I smile. 'It's fine. I don't mind you reminding me.'

All positive encouraging words welcome. And likely required. So, keep speaking them Ed.

He pauses for a little while before speaking again.

'If, for some reason you do find it tough though, or things get weird, let me know ok? Let me help.'

Ed knows. I mean, he doesn't know know. The full facts elude him. I can barely understand it myself, therefore, trying to translate it to someone else seems a somewhat impossible task. But he knows things aren't quite as they should be for me. And he is often strangely aware of when he needs to offer his help.

Even when I think I'm bringing out my best hiding skills, he has this beautiful ability to sense my internal distress.

'Ok. Thanks. I'm sure I'll be fine.' Not sure. No surety whatsoever. But this seems like the best response.

'We don't always have to hang out in a big group either. You don't have to be around loads of people all the time. We can go do some exploring just us two. Or just you by yourself. Whatever you need.'

He's sweet to say this. He knows part of my struggle is being around lots of people for large amounts of time. And I know that when I do need time by myself, he will simply accept it. He won't get annoyed, he won't judge me, he won't take any offense. He will just let me be.

Sadly, his reaction is a minority one.

Chapter 19

We arrive at Sydney Kingsford Smith Airport early on Friday morning, the company having kindly timed it so we'd have a long weekend to rest and be tourists before starting work. In the taxi ride to the hotel, conversation turns to plans for the next few days.

'I have booked us all in to go kayaking first thing tomorrow morning. It will be refreshing to get up early and go out onto the beautiful sea don't you think?' Sally instructs more than asks.

'Thanks Sally, but kayaking isn't really my thing, so I'll just watch from the shore.' I respond.

'How exactly do you know it's not your thing? Have you been before?'

'Well, no, but I'm just pretty sure it's not something I'll enjoy.'

'But how can you be sure of that? If you've never tried it? You can't be sure, surely?' Sally isn't in the mood for backing down easily on this. Please don't let this be how this trip goes.

'Relax Sal, I'm not all that up for it either so I'll hang back with Ames.' Nathan interjects. 'We can go scout out a cool place to have breakfast when you guys are finished.'

There is a pause which she is likely using to decide whether to continue challenging me. She thankfully seems to conclude it's not worth it and responds with a simple 'Fine.' There's eye rolling going on, I'm almost certain of it, despite not being able to see her face.

The words 'I'll do the next activity' waver in my thoughts but I decide not to voice them. I would just be setting myself up for a likely repeat of this depressing conversation, only providing Sally with additional evidence for disappointment.

Instead I stay quiet and shoot Nathan a thankful smile, hoping I really can muster up some ability to participate in the next activity.

I suspect Nathan probably would actually like to go kayaking but is just being really kind by trying to defuse the conversation. I want to tell him that he does not need to babysit me but now is not the time to tell him this. I strongly sense it would not be wise to keep this conversation subject alive. I make a mental note to tell him later instead.

The day passes in a bit of a fog consisting of trying to get our bearings and trying to stay awake to beat the jet lag. Everyone agrees we should just drop our stuff at the hotel then keep moving otherwise the beds might be too tempting and we'll fail the jet lag test.

Our hotel is centrally located in the central business district (or the CBD as it is referred to) so there's plenty to explore nearby wandering the local streets. We wander, we eat, we drink, and we take in some sights. I'm not sure how much we're actually taking in given the slight weirdness we're all feeling after the vast travel, but still, I think it is a fairly pleasant day.

We all successfully make it to the end of the day without having given in to sleep, but there is no resistance or complaint from anyone when it is suggested we all head to our rooms straight after we've finished dinner.

I'm completely exhausted but my brain will not allow slowing down yet. There is still a lot of work to be done before I can even contemplate falling asleep.

Work that is required in order to get used to my hotel room. It is going to be my home for the next two weeks, so I need to make it resemble some level of comfort. We need to somehow become friends because I need this to be my space where I can come and escape and hopefully find some feeling of calm.

This is not a very easy task and I am aware that the maximum level of comfort I can possibly reach here is still pretty low. But I have to work with what I've got so I set about my tasks.

I start assessing and scanning.

Any item I might need to touch will need to be cleaned and wiped down with tissues.

Any visible stains anywhere will need to be noted and committed to memory to ensure I avoid the area.

I need to assess for the most suitable location for my suitcase to stay to keep my belongings safe. (I will likely change my mind on this multiple times and become increasingly annoyed and irate with myself.)

And on. And on… These few items are the mere beginning of my ridiculously long to-do list.

The others no doubt simply collapsed on their beds and are fast asleep by now. I have quite a while to go yet before I'm allowed that luxury. I feel a wave of envy.

My body is aching for sleep. My mind is aching for comfort.

I guess I should be thankful that one at least will eventually be attained despite some delay.

Chapter 20

When I meet up with the others the following morning, I spot my moment to quietly speak to Nathan.

'I thought you would have wanted to go kayaking? Please don't not do it because of me.'

'Surfing is more my thing, I'll definitely do that but I'm honestly happy to give kayaking a miss. Plus, it'll be nice to hang out just us two for a bit.'

'Ok, well only if you're sure. I would be absolutely fine on my own so really, please don't feel you need to miss out just for my benefit.'

'I don't feel I'm missing out. You are not getting rid of me so let's go.'

I smile. 'Ok, let's go.'

It soon becomes clear we are spoilt for choice in finding somewhere for breakfast. We agree on a place pretty quickly and settle ourselves in to a table outside. It's not long before conversation turns to our wonder at the view in front of us.

'So stunning right? The sand, the ocean, the trees – all of it combined into one blissful sight.' We sit a little while in silence just taking it all in before Nathan continues, 'I could have done with living next to this a few years back when I wasn't working for six months.'

'Six months? How come you were so long not working? I can't imagine you taking that much time off. You love what you do.'

'It wasn't exactly through choice.' He looks at me as though he's debating on whether to continue but seems to decide why not. 'I got a bit messed up with depression and had to be signed off work.'

'Oh. Shit Nathan, sorry to hear that.'

'Thanks.'

'You always seem so happy though.'

As soon as the words have left my mouth, I realise what a silly thing this is to say. I know it doesn't work that way.

Almost in unison with my thinking Nathan replies, 'Doesn't seem to work that way.'

'Did something happen to trigger it?'

'No. That was the hard part to get my head

around. You know my brain, I need logic. And there was none. I had a good life – good job, good relationship, slightly questionable flatmates but nothing that was causing too much distress.' He smiles.

'It just seemed to come out of nowhere. I lost ability to see the good in all the good things in my life. I twisted them all up in my head to make them bad instead. Seemed like that was then all I could focus on. I didn't want to get out of bed, I didn't want to shower, I certainly didn't want to leave the house. And so, I didn't do any of those things. I just sort of gave in and gave up.'

It's breaking my heart imagining him in this state. I love how enthusiastic about life he has always been since I've known him. My days find some brightness with his infectious laughter. He seems sort of bathed in a light floaty happiness all the time that I'm addicted to being near.

'That sounds really horrible. What got you through it?'

'My brother.' He answers without hesitation. 'I'd go as far as saying I owe the guy my life. He held on tight and wouldn't stop pulling me up until I got out the other side. I was pretty horrible to him as well. But he completely ignored that and stuck with me. Anything he could think of doing to help he did it.'

Thank you Nathan's brother. Thank you,

thank you, thank you.

'How did he know what would help?'

'He didn't. We've talked about it since and I realise now how freaked out he was about it all. He said he had absolutely no idea what to do. The only one thing he knew for sure was that I needed him, and as much as I turned him away, leaving me to somehow fix myself alone was not the right thing to do. So, despite some horrendous fights, he stayed by my side dragging me through it and we eventually figured out the right things to help me get better.'

'Has it ever happened again?'

'No. Hoping it was just a one-off six-month stand.'

I smile. 'I hope so too, but I guess it must be on your mind sometimes, given you had no warning.'

'Not really. I mean I could go that route but that would just put a dampener on life wouldn't it. In the words of a cheesy self-help quote... why ruin today thinking about a future that might never happen.'

I laugh. 'It might be cheesy but it's very good advice. I think you are wise in listening to it.'

I am actually quite the fan of a positive quote. Many get recited so often they sometimes lose their sparkle but when you stop and truly consider the words, they can give you a mini boost and I'll take any little boost I can get.

The others are approaching so I quickly add, 'I'm glad you told me.'

'I'm glad I told you too.' He smiles.

Chapter 21

Once everyone is settled and has ordered their breakfast, Sally talks endlessly about how amazing the kayaking was and how it's so great to try new things. She seems to be regaling every single detail of her 'special experience' so I soon stop listening.

I'm glad she enjoyed it. I know, however, that her words are for my benefit. I need to let them wash over me. I am beat up enough. I don't need extra hits.

Ed and Nathan both sense what she is doing so each try and change the subject. She's not making it easy for them though. Eventually they are successful, but I have a feeling this will not be the last I hear of how important she thinks it is to try new things.

I feel like screaming at her 'I don't need you to teach me this, I am aware and fully agree it is important. I just don't actually have much of a say in the matter when it comes to deciding whether to do it or not!' But screaming at her would be misdirecting my anger again. My argument would make no sense to her anyway, so adding to the increasing tension is all I would likely achieve.

So, I keep my screams silent. Hidden along with everything else.

The weekend continues on in accompaniment of jet lag and sightseeing. Or maybe better described as bar seeing.

Since the plane kept most of our energy we need to stop and rest a lot until we can accumulate some back. Resting with alcohol seems to be the preferred option for most. It's very relaxed drinking though – outside in the sun, everyone getting on well. No one particularly (or offensively) drunk.

I have somehow managed not to dwell too much on the kayaking saga and notice instead that I am nearing a relaxed state. I am limited to being on the edge of it of course. I know I won't be allowed in but just being able to stand around the edge is pretty good.

It's such a rarity these days I almost don't recognise the feeling. It would be presumptuous and completely false to assume this feeling will last the whole trip, but any time experiencing it at all I am extremely grateful for.

The weekend draws to a close with an enjoyable meal out in one of Ed's suggested restaurants.

'I wasn't too sure if it would still actually be here, given how restaurants don't always stick around that long. Even the good ones. I'm really glad it is though, I used to come here all the time.' He informs me as we're leaving and starting our walk back to the hotel.

'Good memories then?'

'Some good. Some not so good. I had quite an awkwardly bad date here once.' He smiles.

'Ah. Well, it's good you didn't hold it against the restaurant. The food was really great, and it has a nice atmosphere. Very laid back and comfortable.'

'It is isn't it. I think that's why I picked it for a date. But it turned out I maybe should have spent more time picking the person I was on the date with...'

I laugh. 'Maybe.'

'That reminds me actually about something. Ben has been mentioning you quite a bit recently. I think you might have a little admirer there you know.'

Oh. I think I might be a little admirer of Ben too. My soul feels something when I speak to him. As though it's excitedly wondering if it's in the vicinity of a friend.

'What exactly has he been saying?'

'Asking the important facts mainly – Single? Straight? Potential to be a psycho girlfriend?'

'And your response was?'

'Yes. Yes. High potential but totally worth it.'

I smile. He's joking, but unfortunately entirely accurate in saying high potential. I think it would be generous to even consider the word potential really since it's pretty much a given.

'You probably misinterpreted his questions. Ben and I just think of each other as friends. Same as you and me.'

Not same. But I need to focus on making it the same.

'Well, that might be how you feel but Ben is for sure giving different vibes. Would you go on a date with him if he asked?'

'Erm, no. That will not be happening.'

'Why not? You like him enough as a friend, would it not be worth seeing if it could be something more?'

'I just don't have that feeling with him. Now can we drop it please?'

He turns to look at me and I see a fleeting look of confusion before he continues, 'Ok, but I think you might be missing out. Ben is really great.

And you are really great. So, I'm almost certain you would therefore be really great together.'

'Impeccable logic there Ed, but as I've said, I'm just not interested.'

He looks at me intently as though he wants to say something further on the topic but then seems to decide against it. Instead he complies with my request and changes the subject.

Chapter 22

The Sydney office is based in an area called Surry Hills. It's not too far from our hotel so we can walk there, and I am thankfully spared the trauma public transport lays upon me. There could very well be impeccable public transport in Sydney, but it still wouldn't do much to alleviate my concerns. The only thing possible to alleviate them is non-participation.

The office is a converted warehouse building transformed into the requisite trendiness. Again with the open plan but it feels more vast and appealing. Desks are more spread out and there somehow appears more air to breathe.

The first day flies by with getting to know our Sydney colleagues. I have had contact with a few of them when working on past projects so it's good to put faces to emails.

We have lunch in a nearby pub sitting in a

beautiful outside garden area. The sun is shining, and I feel it absorb into my brain.

Sun makes me feel something resembling happy. It's warm. It's bright. It's the happy colour yellow. It feels like the world is giving me a hug when the sun is out, and this is one kind of hug I can actually accept. So, I sit a little while just me and the sun and thank it for appearing today.

I am sitting next to Josh who I know quite well despite him living in Sydney. He spent a few months working in our London office and we came to be quite good friends.

'Reacquainting yourself with that thing in the sky I see.' He smiles.

'I wasn't sure I'd ever see it again.'

'Well I'm glad it's made an appearance today for you. We've had some pretty bad rain the past few weeks.'

'Has it been making you miss London?'

'Ha. No. I definitely do not miss the rain. But I do sometimes miss London as a place, it was fun living there. Sometimes I think about moving there for longer.'

'Really? Have you seen where you currently live?'

He smiles, 'I know, I'm lucky to live in this amazing place but I grew up here, and I guess you always wonder about what life would be like living in different countries.'

I do wonder. I have always wondered.

I always wanted to live in a different country. Not just one but multiple. I remember contemplating when I was very young how a person was to decide which country to live in if they didn't go and try lots first. I obviously had no awareness of such things as visas and legal restrictions at that point and firmly believed this was what I would do once I was old enough. Live in as many different countries as possible before I found the one I wanted to stay in.

I was not to know that a restriction of a different kind would appear as a greater obstacle in preventing me.

Chapter 23

The following day Sally and I are on a coffee run and conversation turns to how good looking she thinks everyone is in the Sydney office. 'I mean, I almost wish I was single. There are some seriously beautiful people here.'

I smile. 'I guess so. Just keep reminding yourself of the beautiful person you have of your very own back home.'

'Oh yes, of course. I know how lucky I am don't worry. But for you – you could do worse than explore the options here.'

'Oh, I don't think so. I'm sure they're all lovely guys but I'm not really looking.'

She looks at me with a mixture of confusion and irritation.

'Why not Amy? I don't get it.' She pauses before continuing. 'Well, actually I do get it. You can't pine for Ed forever you know.'

She most definitely doesn't get it.

'I'm not pining for Ed.'

'Ok... you tell yourself that. But it's pretty obvious to the rest of us.'

This saddens me. But I'd probably assume the same if I was them. It's a far more straightforward explanation.

I decide to change the subject as I know there isn't really any way for me to change her mind.

The first week largely passes in a pattern of work during the day and sampling bars and restaurants during the evening. It's all thankfully presenting as manageable enough activities for me, so I get through them ok.

Despite it all being manageable I still have my regular wobbles of course. I wake one morning and am immediately aware it is in full force mode today. Great.

Back at home I would likely work from home when I am alerted to its strength, but that is not an option here. I'm going to need to bear the force and hope it might weaken as the day goes on. Sometimes it does, sometimes it doesn't. I have no say either way.

I carry out my usual morning routine of showering, getting dressed, and getting ready to leave but everything is taking a long time. Did I use shampoo when I washed my hair? I'm sure I picked up the shampoo bottle but maybe that is yesterday's memory? I better wash my hair again.

Did I wash my hands after opening the curtains? I better go and wash them again just in case. Even though I can see my hands are wet and I am standing by the wash basin.

The 'Did I' questions are numerous and tedious but I am powerless to stop engaging with them.

Ed sends me a message.

Hey, I'm downstairs, the others have gone on ahead.

I'm grateful at least I am not holding up everyone. Holding up one person is still bad of course, but I have to try and grasp at any positives no matter how small.

I quickly reply.

Sorry, won't be long.

Now I feel rushed. Instead of this hurrying me along, all this actually does is cause my brain to think I will make mistakes so the 'Did I' questions multiply further. I am now almost certainly going to take even longer.

Shit, we are going to be so late.

It is quite a while before I can convince

myself that I have done everything deemed necessary in order to leave the room.

I am full of apologies when I meet Ed. He simply brushes them off with kind words said with genuine feeling.

'Don't worry about it.'

If only.

We eventually arrive at the office and Sally is immediately on us.

'Decided to show up then did you?'

'Sorry, I think jet lag is still messing me about. I completely slept through my alarm.' A very plausible excuse despite being very much a lie.

No one in the Sydney office seems too bothered. We thankfully haven't missed any important meetings and one of the managers has not even arrived himself. I am aware that this is not the point though.

Sally is not in the mood to let this go and later on when we are alone at our desks she says, 'You know Amy, it's really rude to be late. These guys are our hosts here and it looks really bad if you just saunter in whenever you feel like it.'

'I know, I didn't do it on purpose.'

'You are always late for stuff though. Even back at home you hardly ever make it to the office on time, do you?'

She's right, I don't. I work late to make up the time, but mornings are not really my friend anymore. We used to have a lovely relationship. I never had a problem waking up early. I'd go to the gym, maybe even do some chores, and still make it into work earlier than most.

Not anymore. I still have no problem waking up early. But productive tasks have been swapped for what my brain assures me are tasks of far greater importance. Tasks that unfortunately have no time attached to them. It doesn't really matter what time I set my alarm, there is no way of knowing when the tasks will be allowed to finish.

So, I am now the friend of lateness.

No, I'm not lazy. Yes, I do value your time. Yes, I am aware my phone tells the time.

I just have no control in conforming to specific set times.

I edit my answer to a shortened, 'I know, I'm rubbish. I do try but I guess I'm just one of those people that is always late.'

'Hm. Guess so. Maybe try not drag Ed down with you though? You could have told him to leave with the rest of us.'

I could have. But I know he would have ignored me and waited anyway. Going back and forth with further text messages arguing the matter would have only delayed things further.

'I am not in control of Ed. He wanted to wait for me, so he waited.'

She's annoying me now. Yes, I'm shit Sally. I know this. You know this. Do we really need to keep going on about it?

'Of course he waited because that's the kind of person he is. Easily taken advantage of.'

I know you want me to bite Sally, but I do not have the energy for this.

'I'm going to go get some water, do you want some?'

She looks at me clearly annoyed that I have ignored her request to build on this argument. But after a pause she reluctantly concedes to give in and answers with a simple 'No.'

Chapter 24

The end of the first week is upon us before we know it. Rob, one of the Sydney guys, informs us that he's having a BBQ at his house in Manly on Saturday and we are all invited. Manly, we are told, is a beautiful beachy suburb a bit further out away from the centre.

'You can drive there if you really wanted but it can be a bit of a nightmare. It's a much better idea to get the ferry.' He says. 'Way more scenic and the Manly ferry is a bit of an institution, so you have to experience it.'

I like boats in principal, so this sounds appealing to me. Or rather, it sounds appealing for all of about one minute, before I am rudely interrupted and reminded to assess for all potential hazards going on a ferry may actually entail.

Somehow, miraculously, I don't let my worries deter me from going though. I'm trying to squash them down in a pile I can hopefully leave at the hotel. This is a dangerous strategy I know as squashed things have a way of springing back up in full force at a later time, but I tell myself I will deal with that later when it happens.

It is taking all my mental strength and I know I'm precariously close to running out, but I keep going anyway.

The ferry trip is only around thirty minutes, so I try and view it just as a long bus ride. The main similarity I am trying to focus on being that I will be able to get off it relatively quickly if I need to. Granted, thirty minutes is quite a long time to be in distress if I were to find myself that way, but at least there is more space to move around so I'm hoping it's worth the risk.

I can change seats without causing too much fuss, or I can even stand outside. My brain seems to accept all this (albeit somewhat loosely) as indicating an ok environment. On account of this, along with being distracted by the beautiful views of Sydney and its suburbs, things don't start off too badly.

We all spread out and Ed and I opt to sit outside. We sit in silence most of the way just taking in what we are seeing and appreciating the beauty of it all. It's proving quite successful at distracting me.

As we turn a corner and Manly comes into

view, we look at each other and smile.

'People actually live here. You know that right? Why are we not doing the same?' he says.

'It would be amazing wouldn't it. Waking up with all this in front of you. Maybe it wouldn't be as special if you saw it every day though.'

'Maybe.' He pauses before adding 'I think we both agree that's pretty doubtful though isn't it?'

'Yes.' I smile.

It has been quite calming being on the sea, however this I suspect has only been a momentary sideshow from my rising encroaching fear. As we approach Manly, I start to recognise the familiar feelings of panic gracing me with their presence.

We are quite far from the hotel and these ferries are not every five minutes. What if I start feeling really uncomfortable and need to leave? What if Rob has planned some activity that I don't want to participate in, and I have to sit looking awkward on the side-lines? What if he doesn't have handwash in his bathroom? The 'what ifs' are gathering speed and I seem powerless to work out how to stop them multiplying.

I'm desperately wishing now that I had stayed back at the hotel. I was trying to trick my brain into pretending it would be ok, but this isn't a situation I'm good at being ok in, why did I think I should attempt it?

I've gone too far now though and the easy option of backing out is no longer within grasp. I need to somehow figure my way through this.

We depart the ferry and make the short walk to Rob's house. I stay entirely silent whilst the others are all chatting in happy moods. I presume they are happy anyway; I'm barely registering any of their words, but the noise of laughter frequently punctuates my awareness, so I think it's a fair assumption.

When we arrive at Rob's house there are lots of people there.

It feels like there are lots of people everywhere in Manly, it's a busy place. I see why. I just wish it wasn't.

Many at the BBQ are from the Sydney office who I've already met, but there's quite a few new people too who I'm being introduced to with extended hands. I'm trying to behave in a socially acceptable way, but I fear my ability may be slipping. I'm finding it an increasing struggle to form a friendly expression and make more than a few words leave my mouth.

Rob goes to greet me with a hug but seems to somehow sense this might not be a good idea and changes tact at the last minute, opting for a brief arm rub instead.

Did I flinch? Did I recoil in horror? Internally certainly, but I plead it wasn't realised externally.

Lots of people here are hugging in greeting. I used to greet friends that way too but now everyone who knows me, knows I am not a hugger. They assume this is just down to me becoming a person who does not like to hug. No underlying disturbing reason, just a person who doesn't enjoy hugging people.

Lots of people fall into this category so it doesn't raise too much concern for weirdness if you confess to it. Unfortunately, I also fall into the much rarer category of not enjoying hugging but also being highly distressed by it.

Even Rob touching me on the arm is spiralling ridiculous thoughts of distress through my head.

I try to push them away, but I feel them taking over. They're strong today. Really strong.

I make pitiful efforts to engage but I'm mostly sat or stood on the periphery of a group. The groups are being loud enough hopefully for no one to notice my silence. They maybe don't even notice my presence. That would be preferable right now.

'You ok?' I turn to see Ed at my side. One person who will always notice.

I make a sound indicating yes and manage a little smile but I'm really not ok. I'm scrambling through thoughts trying to find one that will appear as a valid excuse for me to leave but I can't seem to grab onto any.

'Don't you want?' he asks.

Can he read my thoughts? Does he know I want to leave?

He's waving something at me though. I soon register it as a bottle of beer.

'Oh, um, sure, thanks.'

Maybe alcohol will help. I drink it but it doesn't taste right. I've been drinking this same brand of beer since we got here and enjoyed it, but right now it doesn't taste like it has before. Maybe it's a bad batch. I'm pretty sure that's not the reason though so I don't even bother checking for Ed's opinion.

He makes attempts at conversation, but I can't really focus on what he's saying. I give disappointing one-word answers, hoping they make some kind of sense. The look on his face implies not.

Eventually I relieve him of this agony and excuse myself to the bathroom.

I stare in the mirror and scream words at myself. Inside voice screaming only. I'm sure I'm being weird enough without making things worse by bathroom screaming.

Why can't you do this Amy? Engage, have

fun. Everyone else is finding it pretty easy. You are not being asked to swim with sharks with no protective cage around you. You are at a fricking BBQ with lots of friends and potential to make lots of new friends.

There is nice drink. There is nice food. There is nice conversation. There are nice people. Why can't you focus on that instead of all the other thoughts. WHAT THE HELL IS WRONG WITH YOU.

The screaming was perhaps not the wisest choice. I feel too weak for tough love. Tears start to collect in my eyes.

Great Amy – add to this ridiculousness by having a pathetic cry.

You better have tissues with you because in no uncertain terms are you using anything in here.

Can you just leave me alone? I plead. *I don't want you in my life. I don't know why you appeared. I can't cope with you being here. It's so hard. Are you some kind of life test I am failing miserably at? Because I'm fine with accepting I've failed if we can just move on now and you go. Am I being punished for something?*

I'm here to help protect you remember? It's a good thing I'm here! Otherwise you would have taken all sorts of silly risks and ended up in serious trouble. You have to listen to me Amy or something really bad will happen. That is an absolute fact ok? We can be friends. You just have to listen and follow everything I say.

But you are ruining my life.

No I'm not. I'm saving your life.

I don't want the life you're saving.

Charming. Shall I go and get my friend? It's pretty fond of hanging out with you too. You guys can come to some arrangement if you really don't want me to save you anymore.

No, stop. Please no. I can't have it here in Australia. That's not fair.

Fair? What is that word? I don't understand.

I don't understand you.

You don't need to understand. Like I said, you just need to follow my instructions. It really is the only thing that will keep you safe. Now, do you want to stay in here longer making yourself look even weirder or do you want to just do as I say and then get back out there? You'll feel much better once you do what I tell you to do, I promise.

I'm not sure I will.

I just promised didn't I? There is absolutely no other way you will feel better. You must do as I say. It is the only way. You will be in grave danger if you don't. But if you want to feel all that fear rushing through your body before the inevitable damage beyond repair then fine, go ahead. I'll be here when you change your mind. We both know you will eventually change your mind so I'm not sure why we're even having this argument.

I'm never going to win.

Fine, I will follow your instructions.

Good. Wash your hands. And then the tissues. Don't forget to use your tissues to open the door.

I listlessly follow the instructions then take some deep breathes and re-join the others. I try a bit harder to engage but it still seems to be so far from my capabilities today. It's just not working. I'm relieved when people start to leave, and the day finally drags to an end.

I am not going to be able to leave without yet more challenge though. There is no respite. None today, none any day. The challenges are endless, and today is no different. The only thing that differs is my energy in dealing with them and today energy has all but evaded me.

One of the girls from the office has made us each a miniature, very cool looking and incredibly thoughtful, ornament type thing as a token of memorabilia from our trip.

She looks at us apologetically and as she hands them out says, 'I hope you guys don't think it's too daggy or like tourist tat, I was just feeling creative and thought it might be a nice idea.'

It doesn't match either description, it is

genuinely beautiful, and I would happily place it in my home as a beautiful reminder of this trip.

If that were at all possible. Which it isn't.

It's small enough to fit in my bag but there is of course no way I can put it in there. I can't have this unknown object coming into contact with my other possessions.

I can't reject it and give it back to her as that would be one step too far on the rudeness scale. So, I carry it in the most awkward unnatural way instead. A way that allows minimal contact with my skin. A way that makes me undoubtedly look weird.

I couldn't think of any better option, so I just have to hope that no one notices. They likely will notice but I have to take that risk as I simply can't seem to allow myself to hold this object in a normal way.

Is this another test? Please can we stop with the testing. It's too much today. Way too much. I need out of this test right now.

You shouldn't have even accepted the gift. Goodness knows what you are exposing yourself to! You need to get rid of it as soon as possible. Then afterwards you must spend hours considering how careless you've been as penance.

On the ferry back Sally instructs to us all the plans for the following day. I don't pay too much attention, partly because I have very little available attention to give, but also because I know I won't be participating.

It's too much in this moment to think up a plausible excuse and voice it to her. I know I can't face that confrontation right now. I need to get my brain to sleep as fast as possible and not engage in any further upset beyond what it has already been subjected to. So, I stay quiet simply gazing out to sea.

As soon as we reach the hotel, I make no attempt at prolonging things any further and quickly say my goodbyes before heading straight up to my room.

The first thing I do on entering is throw the beautiful gift in the bin. Then wash my hands. Then wash my hands again. Then wash my hands again. And again.

Chapter 25

The next morning, I wake knowing my first task is to get the excuse out of the way. It is of course Sally I should be letting know directly since it's her plans I'm excusing myself from, but hearing her response doesn't feel like something I can feasibly cope with at all right now. I need to take the easier way.

It doesn't even feel like a choice, it's the only way that presents itself to me. Hearing Sally's anger or disappointment or indifference could possibly tip the balance of my precariously held together emotional state, so I instinctively know I can't have contact with her right now.

I message Ed instead.

I'm not feeling so great, think I need to just hang at the hotel today sorry.

Oh no, I wondered if maybe you weren't doing so good. I was a bit worried about you yesterday. I can hang back too if you want some company?

That's sweet of you to offer thanks, but I think I just need to sleep. I'll be ok on my own – can you let the others know?

Ok, if you're sure. I'll check in with you later – call me if you start feeling worse. Or if you change your mind about company.

I'm grateful he doesn't push it any further.

I do sleep a little, but I largely spend the day reading and pottering. I just know I need this space to be by myself. Things will get worse if I don't do it so I'm being sensible really.

I convince myself my absence is simply best all round. The others won't even notice I'm not there. If I had somehow managed to force myself to go, they almost certainly would notice I was there as it likely wouldn't be pretty.

There is no break from my brain. But I can limit the level of challenge I have to face in some small degree. In order to do that I need to be myself and choose only activities I'm happy attempting. I know I can stop the activity at any moment and not have to come up with an excuse or feel bad for ruining someone else's time.

So, it might still be a rough day but likely far less so than if I force myself to keep going with being around other people.

I decide to go for a walk in the Botanical Gardens in the afternoon. I persuade myself to venture outside for this as it's not too far from the hotel and if it's too busy I will just come straight back again. Being around nature sometimes helps when I'm floundering in this state, so I opt to give it a go.

It transpires to be quite a large space with thankfully not all that many people around, so nature ends up being somewhat successful in its calming effect. I find myself in moments managing to daydream instead of anxiety dream.

I could easily use the time to ruminate over the events of the day before. Beat myself up over how I struggled so badly at what would be considered a preposterous thing to struggle with by most.

I am experienced enough now to know that this leads nowhere good. I would be lying if I thought I could escape doing it altogether, it is impossible to barrier out my negative thoughts completely. But whereas a while back I would spend the whole day in this destructive thought pattern, I have now reached a point where I know my survival is so delicately balanced that I need to take extreme care if there is to be any hope of continuing.

So, I allow nature to take over some thoughts and try and attempt some repair. It will only be temporary repair I know, but any kind of repair, even if only short, is of extreme importance.

After a little while of walking I hear my phone buzz with a message. It's Ed.

How are you doing? We're heading back to the hotel soon – hoping you can join us for dinner? Chilled one I promise.

I don't really want to join them for dinner. Ideally, I would spend the whole day by myself, but I don't want Ed to worry. He has no doubt spent the day worrying about me, so I don't want to impact his enjoyment of the evening as well.

I'm doing better thanks. Yes, I'll meet you for dinner.

I'll try anyway.

When the time comes to meet them, I make my way down to the hotel foyer but stop short when I overhear recognisable voices arguing around the corner, just out of sight.

'She does this all the time though. She can't even be bothered to let me know directly and just swans off doing whatever the hell she wants to do.' I hear Sally say.

'It's not like that, she was genuinely not feeling well. I'm sure she was sad to be missing out.' Ed replies.

'You know that's rubbish, I'm sure she

felt perfectly fine. She just didn't fancy what I'd organised, and heaven forbid she participate in something she doesn't want to do for the sake of making her friends happy.'

'She's participated in loads of stuff you've organised, just let this go.'

'Why should I? She seems to get this free pass from all of us for bailing on loads of activities that are important to us and I'm fed up with it.'

'Sally. Seriously, you need to drop this.'

There is a pause where I could take a good guess at the look on Sally's face before she replies, 'Fine. I know I'm wasting my time saying it to you anyway. Nothing can tarnish your view of precious Amy, right?' she remarks cuttingly before I hear her walking off.

I stand frozen to the spot, taking in their words.

Then realise there's more.

'She's saying it harshly but she's not entirely wrong Ed.' It's Nathan's voice. 'Don't get me wrong, I love the girl to bits, but she does bail on a lot of things – work drinks, birthdays, even Sal's fricking wedding. You can't blame Sal for being a bit annoyed.'

'Yeh I know ok, I just also know it's not as straightforward as Sally is making out.'

'No, I imagine it's probably not, but we're

still allowed to feel pissed off about it.'

You most certainly are Nathan. I wish so much you could all know and understand. I wish you could realise the magnitude in difference between the thought that I just can't be bothered and the actual truth of the matter.

I need to stop listening to this. I wander back down the corridor I came from. No, I'm not going to bail on the evening. I'm just going to walk the long way around so I can compose myself before joining them and pretend I haven't just heard their conversation.

Sally's words were indeed harsh to hear but I really can't blame her. If one of my supposed friends was continually letting me down, not showing up, offering no substantial reason, I'm sure I would naturally feel the same disappointment and frustration.

I hate that it makes me behave this way. And I hate that Sally has to experience this behaviour and read it as is presented to her. I can't explain it to her, so this is just how things have to be.

I have to accept this and not let it pull me under as it so easily could. I know I have to do this but actually doing it is not all that easy.

Hopefully dinner will distract me. For a short time at least.

When I eventually reach the foyer the smile on Ed's face makes me feel instantly better. I don't know why he doesn't seem to get as annoyed with me as everyone else does. I'm not going to spend too long questioning it; I hope it never changes. I'm so incredibly grateful for his patience with me.

Sally barely even registers my attendance at dinner. Ed strategically guided us to the opposite end of the table when we arrived at the restaurant, so Sally and I are kept well separated.

I can only hope that some distance and space will help our relationship, but I know I've just added another crack to an almost broken vase.

'Missed you today.' Ed says after we are seated.

I smile. 'What did you all get up to?'

'Ah, nothing too exciting really. You didn't miss much.'

Don't do that Ed. Don't play it down. I want to hear how much you all enjoyed yourselves. I deserve to miss out on a good day when I've let everyone down. Don't treat me any other way.

I try and transmit this to him telepathically then add in words, 'Well, I'm sure you're not being entirely honest with me there.'

He smiles but won't follow my path. 'The Sydney guys are great to work with aren't they.

They have some really awesome ideas. I think this project is going to be a lot of fun.'

Ok fine.

'Yeh, I think so too.'

We continue on discussing the project in more detail and it feels like it's going to be a nice night.

As long as I keep away from Sally.

Chapter 26

The following week passes in much the same way as the first one. I am more familiar with my surroundings so that eases things a little for me. The amount it eases is entirely marginal, but any amount is welcome, so I am still very grateful.

One day Ed and I finish up quite early so decide to take ourselves off to visit the Museum of Contemporary Art.

It's located near Circular Quay where all the ferries arrive and depart from. We stop and watch them for a while.

'For some people here, that's their daily commute you know. Getting a ferry to work.' Ed says.

'It would be a good way to start the workday. And a good way to end it too.'

'Yeh, wouldn't it? No overcrowded stuffy space on a bus or tube to have to endure, you'd be so much more relaxed.'

I probably wouldn't be all that much more relaxed, but I can concede for most people this would be the case.

'Where did you live and work when you were here?'

'I lived in a place called Paddington which is near Surry Hills. My work was all pretty central, so I just walked everywhere.'

I wish I could walk to work. It would make my life so much easier. My daily bus challenge is one I would desperately love to say goodbye to.

He continues, 'We should have a wander round there if we get the time, I think you'd like it. It has a sort of Notting Hill vibe.'

'I'm not sure we will get the time. It's going so fast.'

'I know, I wish we had longer. And that we weren't working every day. We should have extended the trip to have extra holiday time.'

'Maybe there will be more trips and we can do that next time.'

He smiles, 'Hope so. You like the place then?'

'I do yes. Very much.'

We start walking on to the museum. It's not a big place but Ed and I can lose many hours to art exhibitions of any size.

We stand in front of one particular piece and amuse ourselves with stories for how each part could be interpreted. It appears to be made up of lots of different roads or paths.

'I think it's reflecting the artist's frustration at having lost something.' Ed suggests after we've covered a few lighter options.

'Could be. Could be that he's lost his way and these paths are all uncertainties. He can't decide which to take.'

'Yeh, and he's frustrated and scared that he'll choose wrong.'

'All the paths look pretty similar though. So how can he choose?'

'He just has to commit to picking one and hope for the best, I guess. Like in life, sometimes you just have to take a risk and make a decision without really knowing the outcome.'

'How very profound of us. Could well be he just lost his shoes that morning and painted this expressing only thoughts of 'where the hell did I put them?''

Ed laughs. 'Very possibly.'

All too soon we hear the announcement to signal the museum is closing shortly so we unwillingly make our way to the exit, resolving to come back for another visit. Although I'm not sure when given we only have a few days left.

I find myself unexpectantly wishing as Ed had suggested, that we had indeed extended the trip to include more holiday days.

We decide to go for a walk around an area called the Rocks before going back to meet the others at the hotel.

We don't get far though before we bump into them. They seem to have had a similar idea about where to go when they finished work.

Nathan reminds us about the harbour bridge climb some people are doing later when it gets dark. I'd forgotten about this as I declined his offer to join a while back when he was booking it.

This was a tough one for me to decline. I know before I would not have hesitated in agreeing to participate in this. I love heights. I'm not sure why, maybe because it's closer to the sky. It feels like there's more air up high. More space to breathe.

It would be conceivable to think that given my new best friend is fear, the reason I am declining is because I have now grown to become scared of heights.

That is not the reason. I still love heights. I just can't be in a situation with that much lack of control.

I can't be in a line of people all very close to each other, potentially bumping into me.

I can't hold on to anything that I'm sure health and safety will dictate you have to hold on to.

I can't put on safety clothing they will no doubt insist I wear. Clothing that has clothed numerous other strange bodies.

I can't make it stop if I need it to immediately.

I can't.

And so, I don't.

Sally decided it wasn't for her either. Her reasons I think I can safely conclude are nothing remotely like mine. It's nice anyway to have her company when the time comes for the others to leave. We settle ourselves in a bar with a view of the bridge. It's unlikely we will be able to clearly identify anyone, but that won't stop us guessing.

Sally, after confessing that she is really scared of heights says, 'I honestly don't know how anyone views that as fun, I would be petrified, frozen to the spot.'

I smile. 'Just as well you didn't attempt it then.'

'I wonder if some people do react that way though. They might be doing it to challenge themselves and then panic halfway and can't move. I guess the organisers are probably trained to deal with that kind of reaction though.'

'They probably are but that wouldn't offer me much reassurance if I was the one panicking. I can't see any obvious way for them to get you immediately back on the ground.'

'No. You'd still likely have to face walking back down. And aside from the trauma of that, it would be so embarrassing being the freak that had a meltdown and held up everyone else.'

She says this in a jokey manner, but I can't help but feel annoyed at her words. Sometimes I like to believe/pretend that people don't notice weird behaviour; comments like this put a little dent in that belief and I don't want any dents.

'Anyway,' she continues 'Can we change the subject? I am feeling sick just thinking about this.'

I laugh. 'Sure.'

I comply and ask about her husband, 'How is Adrian? Was he ok about you being away for so long?'

Sally and Adrian are the couple that are glued to each other's sides whenever it be at all possible.

'Oh, he's ok. I mean, he definitely wasn't happy about it. It would be easier if we were at least in a vaguely similar time zone. But we'll survive. I do wish he was here though; he'd really love it.'

'I can't quite imagine anyone not loving

Sydney.'

'No, very true. I think I will suggest to him we come back for a visit. Maybe for next year's anniversary or something.'

'Good idea, gives you almost a year to save up.'

Sally and Adrian just recently had an anniversary. I know this not because I have capacity in my brain to remember such dates, but because I was not invited to their celebrations.

They had a big party on a boat and pretty much everyone in the office was invited except for me.

This caused heated arguments between Ed and Sally as he tried in vain to persuade her to invite me, but she simply would not back down.

I completely understood Sally's side and whilst it hurt, I didn't take any real offense. She was over being let down by me. So, she took the route of protecting her own feelings by simply not inviting me.

Some friends give you only so many chances and I think I am close to running out with Sally. I have quite possibly already run out. We are still friends, but our friendship has changed because of my inability to engage in the way she needs me to.

There have just been too many occasions

where I haven't been capable of behaving in an acceptable way for her. She naturally reached the conclusion I didn't care about our friendship. She then went forth and matched this perceived lack of caring with her own.

I cannot and will not blame her. I am simply thankful she still talks to me at all.

Chapter 27

When the others have finished and come and join us, they are unsurprisingly on some kind of high. Nobody froze. Nobody panicked. They all simply enjoyed the experience and felt no other feelings besides awe and happiness.

They recount the experience to us with the kind intention of trying to include us. Not in any way similar to the way Sally approached the kayaking retelling. I find myself desperate to hear their words. I listen intently to every single one and try and relive it through them.

I am so immensely jealous.

Beyond jealous. If a word existed to represent some higher level of standard jealousy, I am that.

I've missed out yet again. I have of course been allowed to watch because it's not cruel enough just to hear about. I maybe couldn't identify who was who, but I knew it was people. People engaging in life, engaging in amazing experiences.

It would have been too dangerous for you Amy. I was protecting you by making you say no.

But they had so much fun and nothing bad happened to them.

They got lucky.

Is it really just luck?

Yes. You would not be so lucky. You are not a lucky person. I need to protect you.

Protect me from fun?

Don't get smart. Protect you from harm. You know you need me.

I'm not really sure I do know that.

Well I know and that's enough for both of us.

You stop me from doing so much though. How can they all be considered dangerous when lots of other people are doing them?

They just are.

That's a terrible argument.

I never pertained to be good at providing reasons. I just know I need to protect you.

Look at the joy on their faces. Will I ever experience that again?

I don't care about joy. I care about keeping you

alive.

> *Alive with no joy.*

> *As I said, I don't care about joy.*

> *This is exhausting. I will never understand.*

> *Fine. We need to stop this now anyway, there's a stain on this seat you are sitting on that needs your attention.*

Chapter 28

The following evening after work some of the Sydney guys mention they are going for a surf and ask if anyone else would like to join.

Sally left early to go and meet up with an old school friend who moved to Sydney a few years ago. Ed and Nathan are up for it though and persuade me to go along and watch.

They are delighted I agree to going along even if only to watch so I don't feel too bad about not participating in the actual surfing. They of course very sweetly ask if I want to surf but by this point no one is expecting any other answer than no.

No one that is except Jess. Jess is a designer in the Sydney office, and we've been getting on well. She has a fun laid back outgoing spirit and we share a similar humour.

I seem to gravitate more towards laid back

people in choosing friends. I imagine it might be because my body is desperately trying to balance out my extreme non laid-backness.

Jess loves surfing and is desperate for me to try it.

'You'll love it Amy, I promise!' she says.

'It does look fun, but I can pretty much guarantee I will be terrible at it. I struggle with balance on dry land so attempting it on top of moving water is really not a good idea.'

She laughs. 'Everyone thinks that at first, but we'll teach you how to do it. Just give it a go. I am not taking no for an answer.'

You don't have to take it. You can leave it on the ground if you really want but it's the only answer that will be offered. However, I keep my answer to a silent smile and hope that she won't be so forceful once we get to the beach.

The chosen surfing location is quite a bit of a drive but the atmosphere in the car is relaxed and happy. No one seems to be suffering from common workday tiredness that usually attacks at this time of day. I'm not sure if this is how it always is but it's hard not to compare lives.

It's sunny, light and warm outside. The beach we eventually arrive at is hard to describe. Even the word stunning seems inadequate to capture its beauty. It's not overly crowded as they've taken us to a less well known one. It's mainly locals here and they're here to surf. Being able to come here regularly after work must surely be a vitamin for the soul.

I manage to appease Jess when we initially arrive with a promise that I will at least think about surfing after I've watched them for a bit first.

I sit on the sand and watch them all and can't help but become mesmerized. It really does look so much fun.

I wasn't lying to Jess about the balance thing – aside from the obvious instability in my brain, I am not overly balanced in main body either, so I do genuinely think I wouldn't be very good at surfing. But I know that would not have stopped me before.

I would have given it a go.

I start to feel the strangest sensation and slowly realise what it is. I've somehow managed to tune into that old part of me I thought had long left my body. The part that was willing to give new things a go. And be excited at the prospect.

As I watch them surf over waves, the sensation glides through me.

It's so distant and vague I almost miss it. But it's there. I can't get near it to fully grasp hold of it so all I can do is notice it and acknowledge it appear then gradually slip away again.

A distant longing to be out there on the waves too.

Jess appears at my side after some time.

'It's amazing out there today!'

I smile. 'It looks it. You're really good, I'm impressed.'

'Thanks. I love it so much. Any chance I get I am out there, so I've had a lot of practice.' The look in her eyes when she looks back out to the ocean is mirroring the feeling I just noticed.

She looks back to me and says, 'So, shall we start our lesson? It's best to start on the beach.'

'Jess, it's so kind of you to offer to teach me but really, I'm fine just watching.'

'Well, tell your face that because the expression I have been seeing was one of wanting desperately to join in.'

She reads my face well. Ok, time for some lying. Sorry Jess. I don't want to do this, I really don't but I can see you are not going to let this drop and I don't want it to ruin our new friendship. There is plenty of time for it to be inevitably ruined in the future. Let's try and put that time off a little longer.

'The thing is, I can't swim.'

'Oh, really? How come?'

'I just never learnt.'

'But didn't they teach you at school?'

'Some schools do but mine didn't. We don't have the big free expanse of swimming water that you guys have over here remember.'

She laughs. 'Ah, fair enough then. That's such a shame though! I really wanted you to try it.'

'I know, it is a shame.' The look of disappointment on my face to match these words is entirely genuine.

Now that she has finally accepted there is no point in continuing with trying to persuade me to surf, she changes the subject and we chat for a while longer until the others eventually join us.

Jess has severely cut short her surfing time for me, despite me repeatedly telling her she didn't need to stay with me on the beach. I'm glad she did though as she's fun to talk to, but also because I think it was wise that I had some distraction.

The feeling of longing to be out on the ocean I fear may soon have distorted into some kind of torment.

Ed and Nathan are up with a happiness high on the journey back, so I am treated again to the searing jealousy.

I love seeing my friends happy. I really do. But jealousy seems to make an evil prowl around these moments with increasing frequency.

Chapter 29

All too soon we find ourselves at the end of our two-week visit. It has gone with cliché speed.

The last night of the trip is one of the best. Despite us all feeling a little sad to be going home, we appear to have silently agreed to make the very most of enjoying the night.

When we eventually leave our newly adopted favourite bar, we're all a little inebriated but no one offensively so. Everyone is still making coherent sentences, and no one's face has taken on a pale hue indicating oncoming unpleasantness.

We are on a nice stroll back to the hotel when Ed asks if I fancy a bit of a detour.

'One of the guys in the office was telling me about this place with amazing views of the harbour. It would be good to check it out.'

Alcohol has been kind to me tonight. My waking hours generally exist in a state of perpetual tiredness which I imagine is attributed to the amount of brain energy constantly in use. This sometimes means, however, that when I drink alcohol all it does is tip me over the tiredness threshold. I experience a feeling best described as 'must lie down this immediate second' tired.

Tonight, however, I have been spared this feeling and so happily agree to Ed's suggestion.

We drift away from the others and head off on our detour.

We walk in silence for a little while, content in each other's company and Sydney's streets.

Once we reach the recommended place, we face each other and smile. It is indeed an incredibly beautiful view of the harbour we are rewarded with.

We maintain our silence a little longer just observing our magical surroundings. I feel a very rare wave of peace wash through me.

Ed speaks first. He somewhat sharply breaks the silence with words I would not have even vaguely guessed at.

'Ebony sometimes thinks we're having an affair.'

Ebony is Ed's wife. Oh. Did I not mention he's married?

Ebony is lovely. I don't see her all that often but when I do, she is always warm and friendly towards me. She always includes me in social occasions. Despite my numerous rejections she doesn't seem deterred to stop inviting me. That could perhaps be Ed's influence, but I get the feeling it's not actually only that.

We get on really well. She is all the things I am not though – relaxed, outgoing, spontaneous, adventurous. Perfect wife material for Ed.

I am very clearly not perfect wife material. Not for Ed. Not for anyone. I honestly cannot imagine why she would ever even faintly worry.

'What? Why the hell would she think that?' I answer genuinely surprised.

'I don't know. I guess maybe because we get on so well and I talk about you a lot. And other people at work make occasional comments that might have gotten back to her.'

'Right.' I did not expect to be having this conversation. 'And how exactly do you respond?'

'I tell her we're just good friends and that I care a great deal about you but it's nothing more than friendship.'

'Good. Because you know that's how I feel about you too right? I would hate if you weren't my friend.'

'I would hate it too.' He pauses before continuing. 'I would hate it if you just weren't on this planet. The planet would be severely missing out. So, don't go leaving it anytime soon ok?'

It sounds like a weird jokey thing to say. But unfortunately, we both know it's not jokey at all.

I said some pretty dark things to Ed a while ago and unsurprisingly he increased his worry for me by quite a substantial amount after that incident.

I had been having a particularly rough time of things and everything seemed to entirely overwhelm me one day. I felt almost certain that I just couldn't be alive anymore. It was too hard. Too excruciatingly painful to be awake, I needed it to stop.

I spend my life feeling as though I am precariously placed on an almost invisible line of safety, surrounded by harm in all directions. Maintaining balance on this line is so far beyond the meaning of exhausting, no word exists for it. The temptation to let myself just fall swarms around me on a regular basis. On a couple of occasions, it has swarmed so near I feel all control leave my body and only some outside force can save me. On this occasion that outside force was Ed.

The week leading up to it I had been incredibly quiet at work and I know now that Ed had noticed and become a little concerned. So, when I phoned in sick to work, he sent me a message as soon as he found out I was not going to be in. Our conversation went something like this:

Hey Amy, are you ok?

No.

I didn't even have the capacity to pretend. The only words and feelings I had access to were negative.

What's wrong? How can I help?

You can't help. No one can.

Let me try. Tell me what's going on?

Just some stuff. Stuff I don't know how to deal with. Or if it's even actually possible to deal with. It's too hard Ed. I can't do it. I really can't. I'm too tired. I can't fight anymore.

I will help you. Whatever it is, we can work out how to deal with it together.

I'm sorry. You've been such an amazing friend to me. Always remember I thought that ok?

Amy, you are scaring me. Can I come over?

I'm not at home.

Where are you?

Sitting on a bench in the park next to where I live.

Do not move. I am leaving now, will be there as soon as I can.

He did just that. It wasn't long before I felt him at my side, and he sat with me on that bench for hours. Dark words and thoughts kept pouring out of my mouth. I'm sure a lot of it made no sense to him, he was no doubt confused as to why I felt such immense sadness. I still couldn't explain anything in understandable detail. But he listened to it all simply letting me talk.

I could feel his incredible pain at hearing what I was saying, yet he did not once try to cut me off with dismissive words such as 'you'll be fine'. Instead he accepted the pain he was feeling and allowed it to continue with my ongoing melancholic words. Almost as if he was trying to draw the pain away from me and into him instead.

He said some really beautiful things to me that day and somehow eventually convinced me that I might actually be able to cope with being alive. For a little while longer anyway.

Understandably this left him a little affected; my fragility now etched into his awareness. He has kept a close eye on me ever since.

Keeping his gaze firmly on the harbour, he continues on, 'You've been amazing on this trip for the most part and I cannot tell you how happy that makes me to see. I just know it's not always like that and I get a bit crushed when I see you struggle.

We talk about a lot but not everything and I just need you to know that you can talk to me about that other stuff too. Any time day or night ok? If you need someone I will always be there. But I suspect it's maybe not me you need to talk to about the other stuff. I can listen of course and try and understand, but I don't think I'd be equipped to properly help. And I wouldn't want to mess it up. So, will you promise me you'll talk to someone who is equipped to properly help?

Because I worry about you a lot. I know I'm probably not meant to talk about it. But I don't want to spend our lives ignoring it and watching you get worse and then one day finding myself with horrific regret at not saying anything.'

These are a lot of words. I'm silent for a little while, contemplating them.

I'm not sure exactly why I've never tried to talk properly to Ed about everything. Maybe it's because I love our friendship and I don't want him to think any differently of me. I don't want him to think I'm too crazy to have as a friend. Or maybe it's because it's just so incredibly hard to explain. Or because I don't want to risk him ever calling some professional to cart me off to some kind of daunting facility.

It's probably all of the above.

I'm not really sure how to respond. I sometimes feel like there are words collecting waiting to be given to Ed. To attempt to let him in. Could he be someone I could talk to about this?

But something always stops me. I always come to the conclusion that letting him in would result in letting him go.

Despite his kind words, I don't think he'd want to stay. He'd come in, have a look around, and decide 'ok, this kind of crazy is not for me, I'm going to get going now.' It feels like too big a risk, so I push the words away.

We sit admiring and absorbing the sight and sound of the ocean waves for a little while. We're sat as close as two people can get to each other without physically touching. I can actually feel the love of our friendship floating in the air around us. It's such an important relationship to me, more than Ed likely realises.

I know it's my turn to speak but I'm struggling to choose how best to respond.

I desperately want to say, 'I'm absolutely fine and don't need any help.' to reassure him but I know it would just be insulting to say since it's so clearly a lie.

Instead I utter the somewhat small insufficient response of 'I'm sorry I cause you so much worry.'

It's not enough. He deserves a better answer, but I can't seem to find one.

It's a little while more before Ed speaks again.

'Sometimes...' he pauses and makes a big sigh before going on, 'Sometimes, I wonder if Ebony is right to have cause for concern.'

I freeze.

'I mean, I really love her, I am certain of that. Our marriage is a happy one. But sometimes I think I feel these things... things for you that confuse me.'

Don't do this Ed. There is nowhere good for his words to lead so I know I have to stop him continuing.

In some warped, messed up way though I find myself wanting to hear them.

He carries on, 'I love you as a friend, you know that. But sometimes I find myself thinking it's more than that. Sometimes I just can't stop thinking about you. About things you've said that make me laugh. About things you've done that surprise me in the most wonderful way. About things that appear on your face in the most beautiful expressions. And I can't stop. I can't stop going over and over in my mind those things about you.'

'Ed, please stop saying these things.' Sense has finally pushed words out my mouth.

'I know, I know, it's wrong. I'm sorry. I should not be thinking these things and I certainly should not be telling you. I don't know why I am. It just feels like I need to get it out – maybe voicing it will make it into less of a thing?'

'Less of a thing? Hmm. Not sure I follow your logic there. I would have gone for 'more of a thing' myself.'

We're both silent for a little while. Seemingly hoping the ocean will advise us on how to move forward if we stare at it for long enough.

'I need us to stay the way we are Ed.' I eventually break the silence. 'I love our friendship so much and that is partly due to the fact it feels safe. You are married, and I am in no way available, so any wonder of it developing into something more has never been an option to consider. Because of that we're allowed to just focus on being great friends to each other.'

I pause before continuing, 'I felt sure that's what it meant anyway. So, if you think you've gone and found a way to invite that option then I'm going to need you to lose it again. Because I can't not have us in my life.'

He turns to look at me and even though I know it might be wiser to keep my view on the ocean, I turn to look at him too. Sadness is in his eyes. Deep resigned sadness.

He is struggling to know how to answer. I feel his struggle. It's etched around us.

He eventually arrives at some words. 'I don't

know if it will be so easy to lose.'

The words hang in the air between us before he adds, 'But I do know that you will always have me ok? As a friend. Our friendship is staying. So, don't worry about that ok?'

I nod slowly, 'Ok'.

I'm not sure it is ok. Not now.

We stay stuck in this moment for a long time. We can't seem to break free from each other's gaze.

'Shit Amy, I wish so much I could hug you at least.'

I desperately wish this too. But maybe in this instance, the fact I can't hug is stepping in and saving us. It still feels cruel though. So much about my world feels cruel.

This is too much. Tears are forming. I know I need to burst this bubble but it's not easy to leave. I slowly get up. 'Come on, we better head back whilst there's still some time left to sleep.'

He's still staring at me, so I turn my gaze to the ocean and wait until he's ready to leave the crumpled bubble too.

Eventually I feel him at my side, and we walk the whole way back in sadness filled silence.

When we reach the hotel, Ed walks me to my room and waits until I've unlocked the door before saying his goodbyes. 'This won't change us Amy, ok? I promise.'

Ed shouldn't make promises either.

I respond in as much a smile as I can muster but it's very much not one of my best. I nod half-heartedly and reply with only, 'See you in the morning.' I close the door.

Now I'm alone, I can't stop them. Tears fall and fall and fall, and I know I have to let them. I won't be able to stop them, so any attempt is entirely futile.

I'm not in love with Ed. But our conversation has triggered something in me. My tears are filled with grief for love my life can't experience.

Please please can you leave me alone? Do you realise how cruel it is to rob me of being allowed to be in love?

I'm not robbing you. You can be in love. You just can't do anything about it.

And that is better how? You might think you are saving me and protecting me, but you can't understand what those things mean.

No. It's you who doesn't understand. You're still alive, aren't you? Do you really think you would have managed that without me? I think not. You can thank me later when you've got over the dramatics. I'm here for your own good Amy. You need to accept

I'm not going anywhere.

I'm not alive though. In body yes, but beyond that is questionable. You are keeping me alive to simply be an observer. What is the point in that other than cruelness?

My task is just to keep you alive. I don't care about the life I'm keeping you alive with.

Clearly.

I lay down and eventually sadness exhausts me into sleep but it's not long before my alarm is ringing to get me up again.

Chapter 30

I set my alarm ridiculously early because I can almost guarantee that packing and leaving my room is going to take a long time. Even longer given additional precarity added to my mental state from the previous evening.

I walk back and forth from the bathroom. Endlessly washing my hands after all the touching of items I'm packing. It's not offering its usual temporary relief feeling today though. A greater feeling is filling my body and it's not allowing many others. Certainly not any of a remotely pleasant nature.

When I eventually manage to exit the room, I am walking along the corridor and spot Nathan walking towards me. He is looking a little on the tired side. Despite no one being offensively drunk last night, I can't imagine many won't be suffering with a hangover this morning.

'Morning Ames. Jeez, you look as bad as I

feel.'

I couldn't really do much to hide the extent of puffiness in my eyes so resigned myself to just accepting and ignoring it instead.

'Thanks. It was the look I was aiming for. You look as bad as you feel too.'

He smiles. 'Good. Now we've established we both look and feel like shit, I was just coming to see if you wanted a hand with your case?'

I suspect someone has instructed him to come and hurry me up more like, but it's still quite sweet he went with a kinder reason for coming to find me.

'That's kind thanks, but I'm good. It has these things called wheels so even someone with my minimal strength can cope.'

He laughs. 'I'm glad. Because I'm not even sure I have minimal strength today to wheel my own case. Last night was fun though wasn't it?'

'It was yes.' Until the last part.

We meet the others in the hotel foyer. I am of course the last one to appear but thankfully I haven't made us late for the flight. I'm not sure Sally would find that something she could quite forgive.

The mood gracing everyone is a subdued one. It's clear that everyone could have done with more sleep, less alcohol, and more willingness to leave this beautiful city.

I'm aware of Ed's presence on the journey to the airport but we don't have any spoken words or eye contact. I am sat next to Nathan and only speak to him when he asks questions, but even he is not all that up for engaging in much conversation.

We mostly all just stare out the taxi windows at Sydney streets, no doubt all feeling sad to be saying goodbye to them.

Ed was right, I really did love Sydney and I'm sad to be leaving. Sad for many reasons, but sad to be leaving this city is definitely one of them.

Chapter 31

Despite sitting next to each other, Ed and I barely speak for the first flight to Singapore. I think we both know the importance of the first real words we speak to each other and are struggling to find the right ones.

Plus, there is not much privacy in conversations on planes and neither of us wants an audience. It would seem people have apparently formed opinions about our friendship that are not the truth, so we do not want to risk perpetuating this.

We have a slightly longer stop in Singapore this time. It is nice to be off the plane for this break, however, I am starting to feel desperation in needing to be back home now. Whilst everyone is distracted with stretching and searching for the nearest toilets, Ed senses his good moment to guide me away without the others noticing our absence.

We walk for a little while before finding a quiet spot by a window looking out into the dark night. The airport has assumed a strange abandoned feeling given the time of day. There is only a fraction of the normal volume of people since it's only long-haul international flights causing any traffic at this time. Not much is really open, and it feels eerily deserted.

'I don't want us to get back without talking some more. I don't want weirdness between us to become a thing.' Ed starts.

'I don't want that either.' I pause before adding, 'I'm just not sure if something is maybe broken though.'

'I'm not sure either.'

I think for a little time before asking, 'Do I need to maybe stay away from you for a bit? I mean, we sit next to each other, so the only way that would really work is if one of us left and got a new job. But I can be the one to leave if you think that's what you need to happen?'

Please don't agree to this absurdity coming out my mouth. It's not that I care about finding another job. I love my job, but I'd find another one to love I'm sure. I just don't want to leave Ed.

'No of course I'm not asking you to find a new job! I would never do that.'

'I know you're not asking. I am suggesting.

And letting you know that it's ok. I'm ok with doing it if you think it's what you need.'

'No. Absolutely not. No one is leaving their job, ok?'

'Ok.' I am relieved. I would have done it if he'd asked me to but I'm very glad he didn't. 'So, what then?'

'I don't know. I haven't really figured out any solution here beyond talking to you. Do you have any ideas that don't involve one of us finding a new job?'

I stare back to the night for a while, looking for inspiration.

'I could start behaving horribly to you? I could say mean things about your clothes, forget to buy you lunch when I've said I'll pick you up something, spread untrue embarrassing gossip about you round the office? That type of thing? Make you wonder what the hell you were thinking having feelings about me?'

He smiles. 'Horrible as those things sound… and really Amy, I think you could have come up with some better suggestions… I know you would be pretending so I'm not sure my brain would be tricked.'

'Hmm. Ok. No to the being horrible.'

'Next idea?'

I think for a while again, but this is hard.

'I really don't know Ed.'

'Well, this is proving to be really successful isn't it.'

'I'm trying to think but maybe it's better you come up with the idea. I will follow whatever you suggest, I promise.'

There I go again; it always seems to fall out my mouth. I wish the word promise could be erased from my vocabulary.

After some time thinking an idea seems to have popped into his head and he says, 'You know, there is actually one thing that might help.'

'Ok great, tell me.'

'Before I do and before you answer, let's just be clear – you promised me, so you have to at least try this yes?'

Oh shit, I am sensing I've got myself into trouble.

I smile and stare out the window a little more, hoping he might show mercy on me and allow me to renege on my promise.

'Please.' He says to bring me back to his gaze.

'Ok fine. I will try. What is it?'

I close my eyes and feign being scared and he laughs. 'It's a good thing and even though I'm pretty sure you won't appreciate that at first, you will in time.'

'Just get on with it and tell me.'

'You have to go on a date with Ben.'

Oh.

I open my eyes and all joking about has left my presence.

'I'm not doing that.'

'Hear me out. If I know you are happily dating someone it will make me happy to see. I won't spend so much time worrying about you and, therefore, won't spend so much time thinking about you. In theory. Plus, if I know you are in a relationship, then that should signal to my brain that it's not appropriate to think of you in any other way than as a friend. Again, in theory.'

I'm silent as I grasp for an argument to counter his theories.

'Please Amy, you did promise you'd try at least. Just go on one date. Don't think beyond that. That's all I will make the promise commit to ok? One date and if you really do hate it then you don't have to go on another.'

I still can't find suitable words.

'I know it will be hard. I don't know all the detail sure, but I know this isn't going to be an easy thing for you. If you try though, if you attempt this then hopefully it will end up being a really good thing for you too?'

I can't really see any way this is going to be a good thing for me. I can almost guarantee it will be a very bad thing for me. But I can see how desperately he wants this. I want more than anything to keep our friendship, so I finally respond with simply 'Ok.'

He looks delighted and completely surprised, 'Thank you. I will make a promise to you too - my promise is that this is going to be a good thing.'

Ed needs to erase the word promise from his vocabulary too.

Chapter 32

A few days after we are back home and back at work, I am in the coffee shop across the road from the office when I spot Ben sitting at a table in the corner.

I have seen him a couple of times since I've been back but have successfully managed to evade actually speaking to him. I know this is bad. I always quite liked our random chats bumping into each other in and around the office, but now they feel like something that should be avoided at all cost.

I almost make it out of the door with my take-away drink when I hear his voice.

'Amy, hey! Come join me?'

'Oh, hi!' I wander over but make no moves to sit down.

'Good to see you back, how was Australia?'

'It was really good. Sydney is such a

beautiful place. Have you ever been?'

'Not to Sydney no, but I have a brother who lives in Melbourne, so I've been there a few times. Awesome place.'

'Oh, that's cool your brother lives there – great place to have an excuse to visit often.'

'In theory yes, but in practice... maybe not so much.'

'How come?'

I realise what he's meaning though before he speaks, and we end up answering in unison, 'The flight.'

We both smile. 'It's pretty heavy going isn't it? Not something anyone wants to face on a regular basis, so I don't get to Melbourne as often as I'd like. Also, my brother has to come here quite a bit with his work, so it tends to be that way round when we get to see each other. His company fly him business class so it's not quite as much of an endurance for him.'

'Ah, fair enough.'

He glances at his phone and looks torn before saying, 'Sorry Amy, I really need to get to a meeting, shall we walk over?'

'Sure.' Part of me is relieved I don't have to stay in his company any longer as I've been dreading it given what Ed has requested of me. I realise, however, that there is another part of me that was actually quite enjoying speaking to him.

As we part at the top of the elevators he stops and says, 'I'd love to hear more about the trip, maybe we could go for a drink sometime soon?'

So close.

I remind myself of Ed's happiness when I agreed. I have to follow through.

'Um… yeh, ok, sure.' It's a little non-committal sounding but I think he's so surprised I've answered in the affirmative that he doesn't really notice.

'Great!' the enthusiasm and happiness behind his answer makes up for what was lacking in mine. Sensing he might need to seize on this opportunity and lock down an actual time he continues, 'Are you free tomorrow night?'

That is soon. I feel like I need more time to prepare. But in actuality, more time is likely not what I need.

I quickly reply before giving my brain too much time to think, 'Yes, tomorrow is fine.' I accompany my answer with as bright a smile as I can manage in attempt to hide the panic prickling through my body.

'Great, I'll message you tomorrow with a time. Enjoy the rest of the day!' He looks at me before leaving as if communicating one additional silent message. His kind eyes connecting with mine and a beautiful smile formed on his face. Then he is gone. I stand still a little longer, letting his smile wash over me. It seems to be confusing the panic and halting it in its tracks. I notice that in this one brief moment I am feeling some vague surprising resemblance of happiness.

When I think about it later, this could just be two mates going for a drink. Nothing date-like about it. If I approach it that way, then it might be enough to get me to turn up and actually go through with it. Of course, I won't tell Ed this, all he needs to know is that I'm following through with my promise.

Later when Nathan and Sally are in a meeting I turn to Ed and fill him in.

'This is great! And so soon too. I thought you'd just keep putting it off, hoping I'd forget.'

'Can't say that thought didn't cross my mind.' And was firmly my plan had Ben not cornered me into forcing the situation. But again, Ed doesn't need to know these details.

'Well, I'm really glad you ignored it.' He smiles and we go back to working.

Things have been ok with us in the few days since we've been back for the most part, but I'd be lying if I said I hadn't noticed a little shift. I feel drawn to analysing little things that happen, wondering about what he is thinking as a result.

We may have a funny conversation and afterwards I will wonder if he's going to replay it in his mind later. Should I have tried to be not funny? I can't help but feel that maybe I need to be more careful with my words and actions. Edit myself in some way.

It is exhausting trying to do this though and I can't imagine in any way sustainable.

Perhaps we just need some time. The non-date with Ben will be a distraction in the meantime.

Chapter 33

The following day I try not think too much. This is obviously quite an optimistic thing to aim for, but I give it my best shot. I make continual attempts to convince myself it's just a normal day. Nothing scary and potentially life ruining happening this evening.

It's proving difficult not to tune into the panic station though.

When Ben messages me a time and place to meet, my hands are hovering over keys to spell out an excuse for not making it. But something is making them freeze in hover state.

I remind myself why I'm doing this. Ed needs this. Our friendship needs this.

I won't let it go any further. I can't. So just one date is probably safe enough. Then I will have kept my promise to Ed, and we can put it all behind us.

Decision made; I type my simple reply. *Sounds good, see you then.*

When the time comes to meet, we both agree it's wiser to walk a little further away from the office and pick a pub that isn't frequented by all our colleagues. We're not trying to hide some illicit affair granted, but neither are we overly keen on being the subject of office gossip tomorrow.

We fall into conversation easily. I don't feel nervous or in any way awkward which is partly to do with how easy he is to be around, but I'm pretty sure it's also because in my head this is very much not a date.

We talk about work. We talk about our families. It goes beyond small talk and it's really nice to get to know him a bit better. We do have quite a bit in common and things just seem to flow well throughout the night.

If this was a first date, then I couldn't hope for anything better conversation wise.

We are back discussing Australia when he decides to show me some photos on his phone of where his brother lives. He moves round to my side of the table to make showing me easier. The space between us keeps lessening and somewhere around photo three appearing I feel our legs touch.

I freeze. But only for a second before I jolt my leg away.

He doesn't mention the fact I have effectively flinched when he tried to touch me, he just thankfully continues with the photos.

It's knocked me though. It's brought me down and I grow quieter and quieter, ensuring I ask him more questions than he asks me, so I don't need to be the focus.

My attention is drifting, likely soon to be lost.

The thing is this. There was a spark. I felt it not when our legs touched. I felt it just when he was sitting across the table from me. That electric charge that leaps through the air linking two people. It was definitely there.

I'm not sure it's possible to be there and only one person feel it so I'm going to assume he felt it too. And is therefore now perplexed when I appeared somewhat disgusted and tried to push it away by moving my leg.

Thankfully this little incident happened towards the end of the night. It's not long before the pub is closing so I can get away from this.

I shouldn't want to get away. It's a clearly confusing reaction. Everyone wants to experience a spark. When it appears you feel excited, you feel hopeful, you feel exuberant happiness. I feel none of those things. A spark is yet one more thing I'm not allowed to engage with. A firmly built barrier is blockading it out.

When we leave, he walks me to find a taxi. Once one is approaching, he turns and says, 'I had a really nice night, I'm glad we did this.'

Before he can add anything alluding to wanting to do it again, I cut him off quickly with 'Yes, it's been really lovely'.

I say a silent 'thank you' to the taxi driver for speedily appearing next to me so I can leave straight after I've answered, adding slightly manically 'See you at work!'.

As the taxi drives off, I don't turn around because I don't need to. I know he's standing looking after me with a confused hurt look on his face. I don't want to see that look. I'm in enough pain.

This would have been so much easier and kinder on both of us if there was no spark.

Not long after I get home a message comes through on my phone.

Did you get home ok?

Don't be nice to me Ben. You're only making this harder.

Yes thanks.

Good. Really did have a good night, hope we can do it again soon.

I don't reply.

Chapter 34

The next day I get in late to work and sit down at my desk to the immediate sense of Ed's desperation in wanting to talk to me.

I really love sitting next to Ed. Today though, I really do not love sitting next to Ed.

I wish I could sit anywhere else but next to Ed. I can feel his impatience at wanting us to be alone so he can question me about last night. It's distracting and annoying. I don't want to have to talk to him about it so I'm in a bad mood.

I take a deliberately long lunch to avoid the situation even longer, but my efforts are wasted as when I eventually return Nathan and Sally are in a meeting.

'Good, you're back. How did it go last night?' I haven't even sat down or attempted to take off my coat before his words fly at me.

I look at him, not really sure how I should

play this. 'It was good. We got on well.'

'Great! That's really great!' he is sounding a little manic. 'But wait, you don't seem very excited about it and you've been in a grump all morning. These are not the signals of love blooming I want to see Amy.'

I sigh. 'I'm sorry to disappoint you but you will not be seeing love blooming between me and Ben.'

'Why not?'

'We got on. We had a fun night. But that was all it was. It won't be going any further.'

'Those are generally indicators of two people who will see each other again though are they not? How did you leave it? Did he ask to see you again?'

'No. We both agreed it made more sense to stay just friends.'

'You both agreed.'

'Yes.'

'Those specific words came out both of your mouths.'

'Sort of.'

Sometimes I hate the fact he knows me so well.

'This isn't making a whole lot of sense to me.'

It's not making sense to me or likely to Ben either, but understandable sense left the building a long time ago.

'Look, I'm sorry this isn't what you wanted to hear, I know you were really hoping it would work out, but it isn't going to.' I'm getting annoyed now that he's pushed me into this situation. 'I need you to drop this now. I've done what you asked, I went on the date and kept my promise so can we just move on?'

He might have pushed me into this situation but really, my annoyance is being misdirected at him.

'Ok, ok, fine. It's just... I'm disappointed. Disappointed for you. And me obviously. But mostly for you.'

I stare at him for a moment. I'm not doing this here. I turn to my screen and start working.

Towards the end of the day Ben sends me a message.

Hey Amy, how's your day been? It's my cousin's birthday tomorrow and he's having a drinks thing – do you fancy coming?

I have something on tomorrow so can't make it I'm afraid.

That's a shame. How about a drink next week instead?

I'm pretty busy at the moment so next week is not great either. Sorry.

I know. The too busy excuse. Poor. But it feels too harsh to just tell him outright I can't see him again.

Over the next few days he tries a couple more times to get in touch, but I respond with similar cold rejections. I hate doing this to him.

I do genuinely really like him, and he is showing interest in feeling the same. I should be feeling happy, excited at the prospect of something new starting. I don't feel any of those things. I feel desperately sad at yet another wonderful life thing I have to watch pass me by.

I suddenly realise that not only am I losing a potentially great relationship, I'm also losing a friend. This is going to change us. Of course it will, why did I not think this through?

Another friend to add to the pile of lost people stolen from me.

Chapter 35

The following week there is another work drinks occasion. I've had an oddly good day so when the time comes for people to leave, I pack up my things and join them. These times are rare but when they do appear, I am so very happy to see them.

Sally is also happy to see them. She seems genuinely delighted when she realises I am walking next to her, actually about to participate in a work social night.

Remember this Sally. I know it's going to be hard to and you probably won't since all the other times cloud your view of me, but try remember this one Sally – I show up when I can.

For the first part of the evening I'm glad I did show up. Everyone is having fun and I feel part of it.

I am aware of Ben being here but we're chatting in different groups so it's a while before we have any contact.

I'm standing at the bar and I suddenly feel his presence next to me.

'Hey Amy, how's things?'

'Good thanks, you?'

'Good too.' He pauses before continuing as if contemplating how to play this. 'Although, I'm struggling to work out something and wondered if you'd care to share your opinion on it? I could use your advice.'

'Ok.' Not sure where he's going with this.

'So, I went on this date last week with this great girl who I really like. I thought the date went pretty well, and I felt sure it would lead to another. But she's been turning down all my suggestions for further dates and I get the feeling might be avoiding me. Do you think I've blown my chances?'

It's nice he's taking this approach. It's relieving any tension. And it means I get to use third person talking.

'Hmm... I'm not sure. Maybe she enjoyed the date but just felt like you'd be better as friends?'

'Maybe.' He looks at me in silence for a moment before continuing, 'It's just... that's not the vibe I was getting.'

'Well your vibe and your date's vibe are not always the same vibe you know.'

'I know.' He smiles before adding, 'But, whilst I might concede there can be different vibes, I'm not so convinced when it comes to sparks.'

I stay silent.

'You see, that was definitely present and I'm almost certain you felt it too. So, can you help me out here and explain to me the just being friends thing?'

Oh. Dropping the third person now. Time to get serious.

'I'm just not looking for a relationship Ben. You're lovely and I had a great time the other night, I really did, but I just can't be in a relationship right now.'

He thinks on this for a little while before responding. 'Whether you are looking for a relationship or not, sometimes they just appear before you. Is it really sensible to turn it down? I mean, sparks are rare right? They get talked about way more often than they're ever actually felt so are you sure you want to just walk away from that? Plus, I'm not proposing marriage here, it doesn't have to be this serious thing. We could just go on another date and see where it leads?'

These are all lovely sensible words and so much of me wants to let him know how much I agree. I would like nothing more than to just go on another date and see where it leads, but the problem I have is that I know where it leads.

There's no mystery for me. It leads nowhere good for either of us.

I decide to change tact as he's clearly going to need a better answer.

'I'm sorry Ben, the main reason I'm not looking for a relationship is not that I just fancy being on my own for a while, it's more down to the fact I'm still in love with my ex.'

Not entirely not true. I will love my ex forever because he existed before. He represents a time in my past when I was free to be in a relationship. And a very beautiful relationship it was. That love will be preserved in my memory forever. So, if it needs to manifest now in Ben thinking it is preventing me from entering into another relationship, then so be it.

'Oh, I didn't realise you'd been seeing someone.' He looks a little deflated now.

'It was a while ago, but it was quite a difficult break up that was ongoing for some time before it was officially over.'

'Sorry to hear that.' He pauses, perhaps trying to think of something further he can say to persuade me before realising there isn't anything. 'I understand. I won't push things any more then, but it's a shame. I really like you Amy – remember that ok? When the time comes that you feel like you can start dating someone, make sure I'm first on the list of suitors please.'

I smile. 'Absolutely, I promise. And Ben... I really am sorry; I shouldn't have agreed to go for drinks with you in the first place.'

'I'm still glad you did. No harm done. Anyway, I better get these drinks back to the others.' He picks up the drinks and moves to walk away before deciding to add, 'Don't forget what I said though.'

I smile and watch him walk away.

I turn to go and join my friends and immediately feel Ed's eyes on me.

Not now Ed.

I sit down next to Sally where there is thankfully one free seat and nowhere near where Ed is sitting.

She pulls me into the conversation, and I stay with her for the rest of the night. She is very clearly drunk and even louder than usual, but she's being quite amusing and being in her company I think is good for me right now.

The night draws to a close and people slowly start to leave. I can't see Ed anywhere so take my chance and say some quick goodbyes before leaving myself.

I'm not quick enough though and just as I'm almost out the door I hear his voice shouting after me. 'Amy, wait!'

Shit.

'I've barely seen you all night and now you're going to leave without saying goodbye?'

'Sorry, I thought you'd already gone.' I lie.

'Ok, well I'm leaving now too anyway so I'll walk you to a taxi.'

'Ok, great.' Not great. I do not want to have this conversation.

'I saw you chatting with Ben at the bar.' Straight in there then.

'Yeh. We're friends remember? Friends chat when they see each other in pubs.'

'Very funny. Thing is Ames, I saw the way you guys were looking at each other. Friends might chat in pubs, but friends certainly don't look at each other with those kinds of looks.'

'I don't know what you're talking about. I think you're imagining things. You've drunk a fair bit so it's not entirely implausible you might have imagined seeing something because you wanted to see it, don't you think?'

'Don't do that. I know what I saw, and I know you know I'm not imagining anything, so just cut the bull and tell me again why you guys are not going on another date?'

I'm silent for a few minutes. I have no valid reason for Ed. Not one I can speak anyway. He would find it pretty hard to believe I'm still in love with my ex given I barely ever mention him. So that excuse is not an option and I seem completely unable to locate any others.

'Look Ed, I did what you asked. I went on a stupid date and that was all I had to do so why can't you let this go?'

'Because I don't understand. You guys clearly really like each other so you need to make me understand why you won't take it further.'

'I'm not going to get into a relationship with someone just to make you feel better ok? I want to make things easier for you, of course I absolutely do. I will do anything else you suggest. But dating Ben is not going to work so please just drop it.'

'Jeez Amy, I'm not asking you to date the guy just for my benefit. Yes, I know what I said in Singapore and I do still believe it will help me. But I want this for you. I want to see you happy. And I just don't know why you don't let yourself try and be happy.'

I am not party to that decision Ed. These words will make even less sense to him, so I feebly respond with silence instead.

'Silence. Great. You're not even going to grace me with some kind of explanation?' He's getting angry now and Ed pretty much never gets angry.

I can't see this leading anywhere good tonight so when I thankfully spot an available taxi,

I flag it down.

'Just go home Ed, we can talk about this another time.'

'We won't though. I want to talk about it now. Why can't we just talk about it now?'

'Because you've had a lot to drink and you're getting angry and I don't want to speak to you like this.'

And I need some time to figure out a better explanation to placate you. I silently add.

He looks exasperated about to launch into further words but stops himself. As though he suddenly becomes aware that any further words are likely ones he will regret. He responds instead with a simple 'Fine.'

He walks off, neglecting to impart his usual beautiful words to the taxi driver of 'make sure she gets home safe mate, precious cargo.'

Ed and I never fight. This does not feel good. I just couldn't find anything to say to stop the night ending up this way.

I sense his anger and annoyance is a build-up of so much more beyond me not going on a second date with Ben.

Please don't let this be you starting to leave me too Ed. Please don't give up on me.

Chapter 36

It's the weekend the day after our argument so at least Ed has a couple of days to calm down. I'm somewhat naively hoping he'll have decided to drop the matter by Monday and things will just go back to normal Amy and Ed.

I consider sending him a message or calling him over the weekend but every time I try to think of what to say, nothing seems to feel right.

I opt to just hope instead that space will resolve the argument and we won't have to discuss it again.

It's an unsettling couple of days for me though, I feel fragility creeping into my friendship with Ed and it doesn't feel good. Not good at all.

So much of my existence is fragile, I can't bear the thought of it affecting Ed too.

Time passes torturously slowly despite my numerous efforts to distract myself with films, books and chores. I feel an overwhelming urge to be in his company. But I also sense he needs space, so I maintain my resolve in not contacting him.

Monday morning finally arrives. I anxiously approach my desk, eager to find out where Ed's head is at, but it's only Sally who is in so far.

'Friday was a fun night wasn't it?' she asks before quickly adding, 'That is an actual question by the way, it's a little hazy what I remember.'

I laugh. 'Yes, it was fun. Drunk Sally was being very amusing. Don't worry though, I promise she wasn't offensive in any way.'

'Ok good.' she looks visibly relieved before continuing, 'I think it was Ed who got me home safely so remind me to thank him whenever he gets back.'

'Um no, not Ed. Maybe Nathan?'

'Oh gosh. Please let it have been Nathan and not some random I hardly know.'

'Wait, what did you mean when Ed gets back? Gets back from where?'

'He phoned in requesting a few days off apparently. I didn't get told the reason.'

Right.

I pick up my phone instinctively to send

him a message but then stop myself. Maybe he's decided two days space was not enough. Maybe he needs more and needs it to be free of any contact from me.

I don't know for sure if his time off is related to our argument on Friday but if it is and this is how he needs to deal with it, then I will go along with it. However intensely hard that may be for me. I put my phone back down on my desk and get on with some work.

It's horrible not knowing though. Work is not the same without him. I keep finding myself turning to speak to him only to be greeted by the sad vision of his empty desk.

Please come back soon Ed.

I'll try harder. I don't know how, but I'll figure it out. I'll be a better friend. Please don't give up on me.

Chapter 37

As the days pass, I find it more and more excruciating trying to work out what I should do. Should I have gotten in touch? Maybe this isn't anything to do with us and something personal has happened that he's needed time off for. Am I being a rubbish friend by not checking up on him?

By late Wednesday afternoon I make the decision to message him. I can't bare not knowing any longer.

Hey, everything ok?

His response comes back within minutes.

Yeh, just some stuff going on with Ebony. It's fine though. Just needed some time off to sort it. I'll be back tomorrow.

Ok good. I mean, hopefully it's not bad stuff he's talking about that's going on with Ebony, but I can't help but feel relieved he isn't taking time off because he's avoiding me.

I'm a little less sure about this though when he appears the next day. He still seems to be angry. He barely says two words to me all day beyond answering work related questions. His presence feels very much distant from me.

Sally is on holiday now for a few days, but Nathan is clearly picking up on the tension.

'You and Ed ok?' he asks me later when we bump into each other getting water.

'Yeh.'

'Hmm… not sure I really believe that. There's a whole heap of tension surrounding our desks and I'm not loving it. Can you figure it out with him please?'

'It's not me. I think he has some stuff going on at home.' Seems like maybe it is a bit me too though.

'Ok well, let's hope it resolves soon because this is a struggle to sit next to.'

'You'll survive I'm sure.' I smile. 'Maybe take him out for a drink or something though tonight? I don't think I'm the friend to help him at the moment.'

'Ok sure, I'll suggest it.'

Ed declines Nathan's offer though and goes straight home.

Nathan shrugs at me after Ed has gone. 'I

tried. Back to you now.'

More days pass and nothing seems to be improving. I've never seen Ed like this before. He's almost cold in his responses to me, and I can feel anger emanating from him as he overreacts to any and every slight annoyance that presents itself to him.

I'm more and more convinced he's decided hating me is the cure for his feelings.

He's out for lunch one day when Nathan wheels himself round to my desk.

'Ok Ames, this has gone on long enough. I think something is going on between you two and I want to help. You know once Sal gets back she will be way more blunt than me, so if you want to spare us all that then work with me here please. So. What can I do?'

'We had a slight disagreement the other night in the pub. I didn't think it was all that big a deal, but I guess maybe I was wrong.'

'What was the disagreement about?'

'Basically, I promised him I would do something. I did the thing I promised. But despite that, he didn't think I tried hard enough so he got angry.'

'Delightfully cryptic Ames, thanks. But ok, I can live without the detail I guess. Do you think you tried hard enough?'

'Yes.'

Do I really think that? I'm not sure. This is sometimes what I think is a big part of my problem. I don't try hard enough. Or rather, I'm not physically able to try hard enough. I'm just simply too weak.

'And did you tell him that?'

'Yes. Well, I think I did. I can't really remember now.'

'Well maybe try telling him again? If you really believe you did your best, then Ed is not going to hold it against you if you couldn't achieve what he wanted you to.'

'I guess.'

'Talk to him, please. Try.' He smiles and wheels himself back round to his desk.

Nathan leaves early that day I'm almost certain to give Ed and I time to speak. He winks his goodbye to me, and I know the silent words behind it are 'Do it now.'

Ok. Here goes.

'Ed, is your head in something, or can we chat?'

He doesn't break stare from his screen but after a painful pause he replies, 'Give me five.'

It's fifteen minutes before he speaks. I am of course counting and each one of those fifteen minutes is excruciating.

He slowly moves over to my desk and says, 'Ok, what's up?'

It's not what's up with me Ed, it's very much what's up with you. But I don't make any jokey comment to this affect because this needs to stay serious.

'Something not good is going on with you and I'm really hating it so can you talk to me please? Let me know what you're thinking and how I can help?'

He looks at me intently for a little while before speaking. His expression is a heavy mixture of sadness, confusion, anger, resigned. He eventually replies with, 'Ebony's been offered a job in Singapore.'

Oh. Not remotely the response I was expecting.

'That's great news! Wow. Good for her, she must be so excited. And you too – what a great opportunity for you guys. Wow. Really, so great!' I genuinely mean all this but I'm cycling fast into manic waffling territory, so I stop at that.

He looks at me a little perplexed. 'Is it great news? You're happy if I leave?'

'Well no, obviously I'm not happy about the you leaving part, but I'm happy for you both if it's something you really want to do.' I pause before asking, 'Is it something you want to do?'

'We always talked about living abroad at some point but now it's actually manifested as an option I'm not so sure how I feel about it. It's a great opportunity sure, and I'm certain we'd love it there and all those good things. But I keep coming back to what I'd be leaving behind. This job, family, friends...'

'Maybe you could keep this job and work remotely?'

'Yeh maybe. I've already asked about it and they've said they'd be willing to try it out. But I'm not sure if it's maybe better to try something new you know?'

'It probably would be. It might be harder to settle when you're still attached to something back here.'

'Yeh.'

'Plus, a new job might be fun. You've worked here quite a while now and whilst I know you love it, expanding your experience would still be a good thing. There are lots of other jobs out there with potential to love just as much.'

'Maybe.'

We look at each other in silence. I know as well as he does that this job is so much more than just the actual work. Besides the obvious importance of our friendship being a factor, we have fun working here. It's a great group of people to work with and that's not always so easy to replicate.

I continue on, 'Leaving friends and family will be tough, but you can make it work. You can visit and video chat and yes, it won't be the same, but you'll make new friends to replace the old. Family is obviously harder to replace but still, people do this all the time and their lives are all the better for it. You will miss people sure, but there will be so much fun exciting new stuff going on that you'll soon get distracted and in time the missing will become less. I know you struggled with it a bit when you lived in Sydney, but Singapore is not quite as far away, plus Ebony will be with you. This is a good thing Ed. I think you should go.'

'Do you really think that or are you just saying it to convince me because you think it's something I need to hear?'

'Bit of both probably.' I smile. 'Of course, for selfish reasons I want you to stay sitting next to me for the rest of our lives but that's not how it works is it. I will miss you terribly but if I know you're happy then it will take a little of the harshness out of the missing.'

'What if I want to stay sitting next to you for the rest of our lives?'

'Then you must refer to my previous

comment – not an option. One of us has to move jobs at some point and this might be the universe letting us know you're the one to go first.'

We stare at each other in silence for a few moments. Are we still talking about jobs? This feels like we're wandering into dangerous territory.

'Well, we're still just in the talking about it phase anyway. Ebony's having her own wobble about it so it might not even happen.'

'So, wait, this is what you've been so angry and grumpy about? I was getting it in my head it was about our argument in the pub.'

'No. I was totally out of order that night Ames, I'm sorry. I thought about it a lot afterwards once I'd sobered up and it was unfair of me to push you. I was going to call and apologise the next day but then Ebony shared her news and I got distracted. Don't get me wrong, I do get frustrated at not understanding sometimes with you, but I had no right to force you into dating Ben. I'm really sorry.'

'It's fine. I know where your intentions were. It just freaked me out a bit seeing you so angry.'

'I know, I don't know why I got like that. Too much to drink probably.'

Yes. Let's stay with the safe too much

alcohol excuse.

Chapter 38

A few weeks pass and I am pottering about my apartment one Saturday when I hear a message come through on my phone. I'm surprised to see Ed's name pop up as we're not usually in touch over weekends.

Hey Amy, I know it's the weekend but any chance we could meet up later today? Really need to talk to you about something.

I'm pretty sure I know what this is about, but I won't press him via phone message.

We have not really spoken much again about Singapore. He needs to make this decision with Ebony. I've felt wary about getting too involved. Despite believing it to be a good thing for him, I'm not sure I could contain my obvious selfish reasons about wanting him to stay. That doesn't feel fair, so I have kept largely silent on the matter unless he has specifically brought it up.

He may have been thinking along the same lines as he has barely mentioned the subject. I think though today we are going to be talking about it.

Sure, where and when shall I meet you?

A couple of hours later we're in a café and after a brief nervous smile and hello, Ed gets straight to it.

'We're going to Singapore.'

Right.

'I had a feeling that might be what this little meet up was going to be about.' I smile.

'I wanted you to be the first to know, before I tell anyone else at work, and it didn't feel right telling you at the office.' He pauses as if to gauge my reaction but I'm not sure I'm having much of one yet. This feels like a delayed reaction situation.

He continues, 'It's been driving us both crazy going back and forth trying to decide but eventually we just figured we might as well give it a go. We can always come back if it doesn't work out. It doesn't have to be forever does it?'

'No. That's a good way to look at it. Just go with no expectations but make the most of the experience and see where it leads.'

'Exactly.'

'So, when will you leave?'

'Ebony has to leave pretty much straight away as she's already delayed the job offer long enough. So, she'll head out first and start getting set up whilst I hang back and tie up stuff that needs to be sorted here. Not sure how long that will take – maybe a month or two?'

This is fast but we probably need it to be.

'Gosh, busy times then. If you need a hand organising anything then just let me know.'

'Thanks. I think I might need to rope in Sal's supreme organisation skills for this one.'

'Good idea.' I smile.

We chat a bit longer but it's sort of feeling a bit fake. We both want to believe this is a good thing to be happening and none of the words coming out of our mouths are fake. But there is sadness swarming in the joy of the words.

I need to leave. I need to absorb this on my own and not let the sadness spill out in front of him.

We say our goodbyes and I walk in the opposite direction of my home. I'm not entirely sure where I'm walking but it feels like this is what I need to be doing right now.

I do want this for Ed. I know it will be a good thing for him and I'm sure will make him happy. I just wish that happiness didn't involve him leaving my life.

Sure, we'll keep in touch via email and video chat, and maybe even make the occasional visit, but I know how these things go. The contact will slowly become less and less until we're phased out of each other's lives completely.

I'm not sure I'm ready to lose him too. He will be the hardest one to lose. I know how lucky I've been to have him as a friend. His patience and kindness towards me have been such beautiful gifts.

I don't know that I'll be lucky enough to experience it again with anyone else. It will be heart-breaking to lose. But I'm still so glad and grateful it existed in my life even if only for a temporary time.

Thank you Ed.

Chapter 39

The days in the lead up to Ed leaving are tough but I know I have to try and savour this time. I sense Ed knows this too so we both embark on happily deluding ourselves that he is not actually leaving.

We simply don't talk about it. If anyone in the office starts discussing it, we change conversation topic as quickly as is politely possible and continue on as if nothing is changing.

We can't waste this time being sad. There will be plenty of time for that after he has left. These are our last days and we need to keep them preserved in reflection of our beautiful friendship.

Time runs out fast on us though and all too soon I find myself sat in the pub for Ed's leaving drinks. I try to take the approach of treating it like any other work drinks night, and not focus at all on the reason we're all here. I know that if I start registering it, I won't get through this night.

It doesn't really work though. I'm not enjoying the night at all. I can't seem to remember how to form sentences to contribute to conversations with people. I'm sure I will be forgiven for this though; I am shown many looks of pity throughout the night by well-meaning friends.

Everyone is sad Ed is leaving, he is well-liked in our office. But people know how close we are, so I am afforded some forgiveness in being a terrible person to converse with right now.

But I stay. I stay for Ed. This night can't be about me.

I desperately want the night to be over though. I know it should be viewed as a night to celebrate our friendships and Ed's time at the company. Ed's time in my life. But I can't seem to view it in any other way than a horrendously sad gathering.

On account of this, as soon as I notice the first people starting to leave towards the end of the night, I take my cue for acceptable departure and make the decision to leave too. I head over to Ed. I don't even bother saying goodbye to anyone else as I know there is no point in even trying.

'Hey, I think I'm going to get going now.'

'Oh right, ok. Let me walk you out.'

We head outside and he walks me to the

end of the road where I will supposedly wait to get a taxi. No taxis pass here so this won't be my final taxi waiting location but it's where Ed and I silently agree we need to be right now. Far enough away from the pub, whilst also being somewhere we both get to walk away from when we get to the final goodbye part.

'Have you had a good night?' I start.

'Yeh, it's been great. I have been feeling the love for sure, it's going to be hard to leave this place.'

'It will be. But once you get to Singapore it will get easier. The hard part is saying goodbye.'

'Am I doing the right thing Ames?' he looks at me with sadness in his eyes.

'Yes.' I don't even hesitate. Not because I'm in any way certain he's doing the right thing, but because I am certain that he needs my answer to be void of hesitation.

'I'll be in touch regularly. You are going to get sick of reading my emails.'

I smile. 'We will stay in touch. But don't focus on that ok? Make this work Ed. To do that you can't spend too much time thinking about everything here. Promise me you will do that.'

He thinks a little while. 'Ok, I will promise, if you promise me something?'

'What is it?'

'Promise me you will never stop trying. I know it's hard for you sometimes. It breaks my heart to see you struggle and I worry about you. Really worry. Sometimes I can't sleep because I think I should be doing something more to help you. And now I'm leaving, and I will have even less ability to help you so I'm going to worry even more. That's why you need to do this one thing for me Amy. You need to promise me you will never stop trying. Under no circumstances are you allowed to give up ok?'

'Ok. I promise.' I say it with meaning I don't feel. I say it solely for Ed. He needs these words right now, so I won't deliberate over saying them. I feel no guilt at lying.

'Good.' He thankfully seems to accept my answer. 'I'm not really that far away though. If you ever need me, I can be back in the time you fall asleep at night to the time you wake up.'

I'm not sure that is an entirely accurate time calculation, but I'm happy to go along with the pretence. 'I know but I'll be fine. Please don't worry about me. I'm sorry I've caused you so much worry, I know I haven't exactly been an easy friend to have. I really appreciate you sticking with me though so thank you.'

'You don't have to thank me for being your friend Amy, you've been a good friend to me too.'

I have been nowhere near as good a friend

to Ed as he has been to me. He will never really know how much he's helped me but it's impossible to explain in words in this moment. Or any moments really. The words 'thank you' don't even come close to expressing the magnitude of gratitude I feel towards this man.

We stare at each other a little while, neither sure how to end the conversation. There are so many more beautiful words we could say to each other about our friendship, but I think that would just make leaving even harder.

'I'm going to walk away now Ed, and so are you.'

He nods slowly in agreement.

Neither of us move.

'Take care of yourself, and I really do hope you guys have an amazing time in Singapore.'

We stand locked in this moment for a while longer before he eventually replies, 'Do not forget your promise.'

We turn and walk away from each other.

Chapter 40

Our little cluster of desks feels horrible and subdued the first day without Ed there. I try to pretend he's just on holiday, but my mind is struggling to be tricked. Nathan tries his best at cheering us with the occasional joke but even Sally is barely breaking a smile.

It carries on like this for a few days when Nathan eventually breaks. 'Guys, this sucks. Really fricking sucks. But we can't sit about like this forever mourning Ed's absence. Anyone got any suggestions for how we can lift the mood a bit?'

'I'm not sure you can force these things Nathan.' Sally says.

She looks at me with compassion filled eyes before adding, 'We'll get there. We just need a bit of time.'

A few days later I get into the office and

notice someone sitting at Ed's desk. Of course they weren't going to leave it empty for long but I don't feel ready to deal with a new neighbour yet. Although, I'm not sure that is something I will ever feel.

'Hi.' I say sitting down.

'Hey. I'm Mark. I'm going to be doing a bit of freelancing for you guys.'

'Oh right, great.' Temporary neighbour then. I'm not sure if I prefer this or not.

I pretend not to see he's holding out his hand for me to shake and take a ridiculous amount of time taking off my coat instead. I don't look in his direction but keep talking to try and hide the rudeness.

'Where have you worked before?' I ask, trying to resemble someone who is interested in his words.

He's a chatty guy and seems friendly enough but I'm not really listening to anything he's saying.

I'm sorry Mark. You don't deserve this.

Work drinks are quickly organised to welcome the new guy but I'm ready with my excuse without even pretending to attempt going.

It's becoming strong again. I know I'm going to need a little time with avoidance.

Sally doesn't even remotely question my excuse. She seems to have taken on a stance of taking pity on me. I imagine because she is currently able to pinpoint a good reason for me fabricating excuses.

I tell myself I will make more of an effort with Mark. Temporary or not, he shouldn't have to be subjected to the mess of a work neighbour I seem to be dissolving into. This effort is elusive to me right now though, so these are merely words marked for me to address in the future.

Days pass but each one seems to bring stronger greater challenges for me.

Is this a new level or something? I thought we were pretty high already.

I'm just sensing you need to take more care since you're distracted thinking about Ed leaving.

It feels like you are just endlessly adding to the list of things you consider dangerous.

I am yes.

But if they weren't dangerous before and didn't cause me any harm, why are they suddenly now?

We hadn't fully assessed them correctly before. We must have just got really lucky for them to not have caused any harm.

I thought you said I wasn't lucky.

You're not.

?

Just stop arguing and follow my instructions. You know you are wasting your time. I will always win.

I know you will. I just don't know why.

A couple of weeks later I'm leaving work in the evening when I bump into Ben on the steps outside our building.

'Hi Amy, how's things?'

'Good thanks.' I lie.

'Great, work keeping you busy?'

'As always. I better get going though, I have something on tonight.' More lies.

'Oh, ok, well I'll see you soon hopefully.'

'Bye.' I manage a small smile at least.

Our interactions since our non-date discussion don't actually appear to have suffered too much damage. His level of friendliness has not diminished and I'm extremely grateful for this. I can't seem to match this friendliness today though. I am feeling familiar end-of-day desperation at wanting to get home.

As I get to the end of the street, I'm not sure

why but something instructs me to turn around and glance back to the office steps. As I do, my vision slowly rests upon Ben embracing a woman. After a brief kiss, they walk off in the opposite direction holding hands.

Well, what did I expect – that he'd wait around for me, possibly forever? Of course he's going to move on. I can't seem to move from this spot staring at them. The vision of a happy couple starts becoming so much more than is presented on the surface.

Before, that would have been me. I'm looking at what's been cruelly stolen from me. And I can't seem to look away.

I have no idea how long I end up standing in that spot for. When I eventually fall back into reality, Ben I'm sure is long gone. The light seems darker though.

I get myself home but it's not a pretty journey. I can't stop the tears from falling and I am no doubt attracting scared/worried/annoyed glances from passers-by, but I have no capacity to care.

Once I finally step through the door of my home, I know I won't be leaving again any time soon.

Chapter 41

Days pass, maybe even weeks, I'm not entirely aware of moving through each day. Nothing is registering much in my conscious hours.

I find myself contemplating how long it might take for it to be over if I just didn't move ever again.

Would it be painful? Would I slip into some delirious state and ruin it by moving? How would I look when someone found me? Would I change the course of the life of the person who found me?

Dark thoughts are my sole companion through these days, until I am woken from sleep one day to loud banging on my door.

I realise it is being joined by shouting.

'Amy, answer the door. It's Nathan. I'm going to keep banging on this door until you answer so if you want to be kind to your neighbours, hurry up.'

What is Nathan doing here? I'm confused. His presence makes no sense to me in this environment.

I don't want to talk to him. I definitely don't want to see him. I stay in bed and try and ignore him.

He's persistent though. Shit Nathan, leave me alone.

He's attempting more words through the letterbox, but I can't really make them out. He is clearly happy to keep this up for a long time, so I eventually give in and go and open the door.

'What the hell Nathan? What are you doing here?' I'm annoyed he has made me exert energy in leaving my bed and answering the door.

'Amy, thank fuck.' His previous words had an edge of jovialness but these three have none.

I stare at him.

He stares back before eventually continuing, 'Everyone's really worried about you, so I had to come check on you.'

'You could have called?'

'I did. I've called loads. So has Sal, so have others at work.'

Work. Shit. The excuse I gave for needing time off has likely run out by now and I've made no attempt at extending it. Did I even call them with an excuse in the first place?

I have no idea how long I've been off for. My brain has stopped registering days. I've been aware of light outside and dark outside, but counting these transitions is beyond my capabilities.

'Oh. I haven't checked my phone in a while.'

'Right. Well, can I come in?'

'No.'

'Amy, I'm worried. Now I've seen you, I'm even more worried. You look like shit. Please just let me in for a little bit? I won't stay, I don't even need to go beyond the hallway. Just let me in so we aren't having this conversation in full view of your neighbours?'

There is no way he is going beyond the hallway, but I open the door to signal my agreement. I don't want to be involved in a scene drawing my neighbour's attention.

'Thanks.' he says as he walks in. Relief at my agreement joining his steps.

I stand in silence.

'Do you want to talk to me about what's going on?'

'No.'

'Ok, well, I've got a pretty good idea. The summary version anyway. When was the last time you left the house?'

I stare blankly. As far as my brain is concerned there is no longer a world outside.

'Right. So, this is what we're going to do. I'm going to make an appointment for you at your doctors and I'm going to drive you there and back. You're not going to think beyond that. This is just one task you have to commit to doing ok? There are no other tasks, nothing to scare yourself with thinking about what will happen after. The only thing you need to focus on is this one task. Can you do that?'

I stare my silent response.

'You have to agree to this Amy. I am not leaving this hallway until you do. So, either you agree, or I will settle myself in nicely for a very long time. Those are your choices.'

Rubbish choices Nathan.

I stare at him some more before I finally concede that agreeing to go to the doctors will be the fastest way to get him to leave. I don't think I've ever seen him this serious before.

'Fine. I will go to the doctors.' I lie.

'Good. Now go and get your phone so I can get the number and make the appointment.'

I sigh. 'I'll send you the number later.'

'No Amy. Go and get it now.'

I try to show annoyance and frustration,

but my body doesn't seem to have the energy to manifest the expression on my face, so I wander off instead to get my phone.

Nathan makes the appointment and instructs he will be back to collect me in two hours.

'What? The appointment is today?'

'Yes. I got one of those same day emergency appointments.'

'I'm not an emergency.'

He looks at me with sadness in his eyes. 'I'll be back in two hours.'

He walks back out to his car, but I don't hear the engine start. I glance out the window ten minutes later and he's still sat there. Great, he thinks I'm going to make some kind of escape. Good thinking Nathan, you're good at this.

I'm probably going to have to go to this appointment then.

I wander in and out of different rooms as though trying to remind myself how to prepare for going outside. I walk past a mirror and realise Nathan's assessment of my appearance is not wrong. But does it actually even matter? I don't make any attempt to address the issue.

When the two hours are up, I open the front door and stand still for a little while. Perhaps I am acclimatising myself to this new type of air.

I breathe in. I breathe out. I breathe in again. I breathe out again. Listen to Nathan, remember his instructions. Just this one task.

I walk slowly out to his car and get in. He looks relieved. Probably because he hasn't had to attempt any kind of force.

I stay pretty much silent for the journey except when he asks, 'Do you want me to come in with you? I mean, I will be in the waiting room with you, but I mean to the actual doctor's room? It's probably best you speak to them by yourself then you can be completely honest and not worry about saying stuff in front of me. But if you just feel like you want a friend next to you, I'll absolutely come in with you. What would you prefer?'

I consider this for a moment before answering, 'I'll go in by myself.'

'Fine. But you have to be totally honest with them ok Ames? That is the most important thing to remember when you're in there. No lies ok?'

I briefly contemplate questioning him about his assumption that lying to a doctor is something I would consider. But I don't have the energy to argue about his entirely accurate assumption. I respond instead with one word, 'Ok.'

We sit in silence in the waiting room and I look around. There's a woman coughing. She looks a bit feverish. I feel a surge of jealousy. When she sees the doctor, they will no doubt simply prescribe her antibiotics. She will then go home and take them, and then soon after she will be fixed.

No awkwardness. Straightforward, common illness. Why can't mine be like that.

When my name is called, I don't hear it. I'm still transfixed in my story about the coughing woman. Eventually Nathan's voice breaks my gaze 'Amy.' 'Ames, it's time now.'

I look at him and slowly nod before rising slowly and walking slowly towards the doctor. All my movements only seem to be aware of one possible pace.

She smiles and indicates for me to follow her along a bright corridor into her room. She closes the door after me and points to a chair for me to sit in whilst sitting in her own chair. But I can't seem to move from near the door.

I don't want to sit in that chair. I think of all the sick people who have sat in that chair. I didn't even want to sit in the waiting room chair. But I did it, and that is now feeling like a bad decision. I wasn't paying enough attention. I should have stayed standing. The fear is starting to seep through me. Here we go again...

This is so exhausting.

'Amy?' she's at my side now offering a box of

tissues. I realise I must be crying.

'Just take your time. When you're ready, explain to me what's going on. Then we'll see how I can help ok?'

I eventually manage to get some words out, but our allotted ten minutes is not going to come anywhere close to being enough time to explain what's going on in my brain.

I get the two important labels out though, so she gets a lead at least on the rest.

'Would you be open to seeing a psychologist Amy?'

'I don't know.'

'I think it would be a good idea. You don't have to keep trying to cope with this by yourself. No harm in giving it a go?'

'Ok.'

'I'd also really like to start you on some medication. Just to help with the mood side of things. Get you able to leave the house again. What do you think?'

'Ok.'

I'm not really sure how I feel about either of these things, 'ok' just seems the easiest word to say right now.

I could keep pretending everything's fine. I could keep hoping it will just resolve itself in time, all I need to do is be patient. But pretending is proving increasingly difficult. And hope is becoming an ever-fading feeling.

I clearly can't fix this by myself. I have no idea what is even really going on in my brain so how can I make any realistic attempt at fixing it?

I need to try something else. So, therapy and medication it is. This is what I will try. If this doesn't work, then I am still left with my one final option. That option might somehow be easier once I know that I truly did try everything that was possible before I arrived there.

I will know this, and others will also know. It might even offer then some ease to be in the knowledge that it really was a last resort. Confirmation that nothing existed to save me so there couldn't be any other way.

Maybe that will offer some kind of peace.

I think of Ed and my promise. This is me trying Ed.

The doctor sends me off with a prescription for the medication, and an instruction to look out for a letter that will detail a psychologist appointment. I re-join Nathan and we head back out to his car.

'How did it go?' he asks once we're sat with closed doors.

'She's given me a prescription for

medication, and she wants me to go to therapy.'

'Ok.' He looks at me and adds, 'These are good things. These are going to get you better. You have to follow through with them though. Can you do that?'

I look out the window at the world I hope to one day be able to join. I sense this is my only chance of that ever becoming an actuality. I answer with what appear to be two recurring important words in my existence.

'I'll try.'

Chapter 42

Nathan isn't taking any chances and stops off at the chemist to ensure I pick up the prescription at least. He follows me in but wanders off to buy some stuff at another counter.

We drive back in silence, my gaze transfixed on the outside world. It's strange to observe after all this time inside. The world is still moving along as it always does. People going about their daily lives. This is how it will be if I get to the final option and leave.

Yes, some people will be sad for a little while. They may be confused. They may be angry. They may be hurt. They may be relieved. They may be all of those things combined, but in time they will go back to being the things they are in their regular daily lives. The things I'm observing through this window. Their lives will go on. In some cases, they will go on perhaps easier given they have been alleviated from a little worry.

I don't want to cause anyone pain. But the magnitude of pain I feel within myself is so overwhelming. Being in my current existence hurts. It hurts so very vastly there are no words that exist to truly depict its measure. I feel so drawn to just making it stop, regardless of any consequences.

I know I am on a precariously flimsy line right now. Are medication and therapy really actually any match for this?

I realise we have arrived back at my apartment and hear Nathan ask, 'Can I come in for a bit? Keep you company – we could watch a movie or something?'

He already knows what my reply is going to be, but I feel something at knowing he asked anyway. Why would he want to spend time with this crazy shell of a person sitting in front of him? I can't understand his presence.

'No, I'll be fine on my own.' Will I?

He also knows not to push it. He's well aware that today has been a big step for me and he has to handle this with care. He's not going to budge on one thing though.

'Ok fine but here, take this.' He passes me a bottle of water. 'Can you take one of the pills now please in front of me? Just so...' he fumbles for further explanation but can't seem to find anything suitable so resorts to simply, 'Please Ames? For me?'

I look into his eyes and realise I don't recognise him. I've never seen this expression on his face before. He looks so desperately anxiously sad.

It's enough to make me push back the argument I was about to voice. Instead I answer simply, 'Ok.'

Remember Amy, you are going to try this. So, start the trying now.

I swallow the pill and get out of the car.

Chapter 43

I do try. The trying really only encompasses two specific tasks but I commit to them. Taking a pill every day and waiting for a letter about a therapist appointment. This is trying I can do. Maybe even be good at. Not the greatest achievement in the world but I'll delude myself.

As it's pretty obvious these two undertakings are the sum of what I can achieve in the days that follow, Nathan takes it upon himself to take on other necessary tasks. Tasks that don't involve him entering my home obviously. He doesn't question this too much thankfully as, like with everything else, I can't explain it to him.

I live in a small one-bedroom apartment. It technically has two bedrooms, but one is so tiny it's insulting really to label it as a bedroom. You could fit a bed in there, but I suspect it would feel similar to sleeping in a cupboard. I have no need for a second bedroom anyway, I am barely allowed guests on the doorstep so sleeping over is entirely out of the question.

I used to love entertaining guests. I lived in a home filled with life. Friends were always coming to visit for dinners or drinks. The atmosphere overflowed with laughter and fun.

Such an atmosphere is entirely alien to my current home. The space overall is small but I don't need a lot of space given I have very little to fill it with. There is no inviting furniture, no space for guests to sit. Aside from the sparse collection of furniture, I don't even own many possessions at all. More possessions just equates to more things to worry about so they are rejected. Just as people are.

So, Nathan is not allowed to enter my apartment.

He brings me food shopping. He takes care of work for me. I don't know what he's told them, but he instructs me not to worry about it. He makes sure my bills are paid.

He sends me a message every morning and every evening to see how I am doing. If I don't answer he will call. If I don't answer his call, he will show up on my doorstep and not leave until he's seen me and spoken to me and I've promised him that I really am ok, and he can leave.

One day we are speaking on the phone and he asks, 'Has the therapist letter arrived yet?'

'No, but I think the doctor said it would take a while. I don't think they send it till a bit nearer the time when the first appointment will actually be.'

'Right. Did she give you an indication of when that might be?'

'She said there is always a waiting list and it might be a few months.'

'A few months? As in three months?'

'I think so, yes.'

'That is ridiculous. You can't wait that long.'

'I'll be fine.'

'Is there no way to speed it up? You did make it clear to her how bad things were didn't you?'

'I guess. I don't know. Maybe lots of other people are bad too. You can speed it up by going to a private therapist I think but then you have to pay.'

'Right. Ok good, I will pay. I will investigate private therapists and get back to you once I've found one. Leave this with me.'

'No! Nathan, you can't do that. You can't pay for my therapy, that is too much.'

'I'm doing this Ames, no arguments.'

He hangs up the phone before I can protest

further. I have no energy for arguing anyway. I will let him do his investigating for now but make sure it goes no further.

Chapter 44

A couple of days later Nathan sends me a message in the morning.

I've made an appointment for you and will drive you there. Be ready at 1.30pm.

I type out numerous variations of a rejection reply but something stops me sending them.

I agreed to try the therapy option and I've been given the chance to start it soon. If I wait three months that is a substantial amount of time to talk myself out of it. I know I could easily slip back into just convincing myself I'm fine. Or worse.

Something tells me that whilst I have any modicum of willingness to try this, I need to act on it.

So, I erase all my initial replies and opt for a simple *Fine* instead.

Nathan arrives promptly at 1.30pm. I am

mostly silent for the drive while I contemplate what is about to happen. I'm not really sure what therapy will actually involve beyond trying to describe what is going on in my brain.

Will I be able to explain it? Will they in any way understand? Will they let me leave at the end or will they have me committed to some terrifying mental facility?

When we reach the appointment location, Nathan parks outside and as I glance at the building I ask him, 'Are you sure this is the right place?'

It looks like an old apartment building. A place where people live, not where they try to fix brains.

'Yeh, this definitely matches the address. I guess they like to make these places discreet.'

They have succeeded. I don't really care though if anyone were to see me. I barely register people in this outside world aside from Nathan. I have no capacity to consider other people and the stories they might be making up in their heads about me.

There is a small plaque on the main door of the building with the therapist's name on it. It's quite camouflaged really, you would only make out the name if you were standing close specifically looking at it.

We are at the right address then.

Nathan is going to pick me up afterwards, but let's me walk into the building alone. I sit in the waiting area and look out of the window. I glance down to the street and notice Nathan's car has not moved.

Maybe he is checking his phone or checking something in the car that needs checking. Something that delays his departure. I have a feeling though he's not doing any of that.

I'm a little early for the appointment. I suspect Nathan deliberately allowed for additional time in case time for persuading was required. I use the wait to productively stare vacantly at the floor.

My staring is interrupted eventually when I hear my name called. I look up and see a man who introduces himself to me as Arthur.

'It's lovely to meet you Amy, come on through.' He doesn't try to shake my hand which I know might seem rude to many, but it's made me instantly like him.

He guides me to his room and indicates a chair for me to sit in. It's one of those tub chairs that look as though they were designed to make you feel like you are being hugged when you sit back in it.

I of course can accept no such hug so sit

perched on the very edge of it instead.

The room is pleasant enough to be in. It appears clean. It's warm without being hot. There is a clock on the wall. It's placed to the side of us, perhaps so as not to be too intrusive on our conversation.

There is a small table between us with two glasses of water. One on Arthur's side and one on mine. In the middle there is a box of tissues. Thoughtful items, none of which I will be allowed to entertain using.

There is some distant noise from traffic outside but aside from that it is quite peaceful.

Arthur begins.

He smiles a warm friendly smile and asks, 'What brings you here today Amy?'

So much. So many things.

I'm not quite sure how to answer this though. I end up opting for just facts.

'My doctor advised it might be a good idea.'

'Ok. Do you want to tell me a bit about what's been going on?'

'I'm not really sure where to start. I mean, I know I have these two things. One thing mainly but then the other sometimes appears. It's here at the moment. It's been quite bad this time, the worst it's ever been really. So, I guess that's what made me end up at the doctors.'

'Can you tell me the names of the two things?'

I know the names well, it's just hard to say them out loud for some reason. As if voicing them gives them some kind of power. As though it brings them into existence. I realise in this moment how ridiculous that is. They have very obviously bulldozed their way into existence in recent years paying no attention whatsoever as to whether I've spoken their names out loud.

I look at him for a little while in silence before making my decision.

'I have OCD.' I clarify by adding 'Obsessive Compulsive Disorder', although I would hope he knows what the acronym stands for, otherwise we are likely wasting our time here. 'And then also sometimes depression.'

It feels strange saying this. I self-diagnosed myself long ago when I could resist the internet no longer. But once I felt I'd found enough to give myself these labels I didn't go any further. It scared me too much.

I feel compelled to add, 'Not the jokey kind of OCD where someone might occasionally double check they've locked a door and say 'I'm so OCD about that door!'. There is nothing remotely jokey about the kind I have. It's taken over my life. It's taken over it and ruined it. Smashed it up into little pieces.'

I continue on and describe to him my existence. It all comes tumbling out my mouth in surprisingly easy fashion. I'm not sure why but I find myself completely able to talk to him about it.

Perhaps it is because I know he is a medical professional, and this is all confidential. He exists only in this. He is not my friend so there is no fear of losing a friendship. He is not my boss so there is no fear of losing my job. He is not someone I will have any contact with outside of this very room, so I feel this is one person that matters not if they judge me. There is little consequence.

I do censor things slightly though at the beginning. I still have some fear that he might decide I am some kind of danger to myself and take some action that will affect things outside of this room. But the more we talk and the more I see expressions on his face (or more accurately, lack of expressions), I am shown more evidence that he is not shocked by my words and he is not going to judge me. He is simply going to listen.

He is going to listen and also show some form of understanding. I have always known there are other people in the world who are like me but still in my existence it has felt unique. Here, in this setting, as he occasionally mentions statistics and experiences of others with similar, I am reminded that he will have heard my story before.

Manifested in a different form of course, but the foundations being the same.

Thank you Arthur, I'm glad I let Nathan talk me into meeting with you.

All too soon I am aware of him glancing at the clock and he informs me that our time is almost up.

'I would like to continue speaking with you Amy. I do think I can help you. I have a fair bit of experience working in these areas so would be happy to work with you. What do you think? Would you like to come back?'

What do I think?

I think this hasn't been so bad. He doesn't appear to be giving any indication that he has phoned for assistance to ensure I am not let back out into the world by myself. He hasn't appeared shocked or confused at any of my words. I have felt compassion in him listening to me which has been comforting to experience. Maybe this could actually help.

'Yes. I think I will come back.'

Chapter 45

As I leave the appointment I walk out onto the street and see Nathan's car parked in exactly the same spot as it was when he dropped me off.

He hasn't moved. I'm sure there were loads of things he could have gone and done in the hour, but he chose to stay in this very spot and wait for me. Just in case.

I get in and smile at him. It's not a smile that quite meets my eyes as I'm simply not capable of such at the moment. But neither is it a smile devoid of any genuine feeling.

We are silent for a while on the drive home. I can tell he wants to ask me how it went but is unsure if he should or not. I consider starting the conversation myself and talking about it, but I think I need to keep it all in Arthur's room for now.

He eventually speaks but decides on a different safer topic confined to the realms of small talk. I am relieved and engage as best I can.

We arrive back at my apartment and as I'm about to get out the car he asks, 'Will you go again? I mean, did you make another appointment?'

'Yes. Same time next week.'

'Great.' he smiles before quickly adding, 'I'll put it in my calendar.'

'Why would you do that?'

'To remind myself to drive you there and back.'

'You don't need to do that.'

'I want to.'

I'm about to protest further but remind myself how much easier he is making my life for me at the moment. Let him do this for you Amy. Let him help. You need all the help you can get.

I nod and reply, 'Ok, if you are sure.'

'I am sure. It's no problem at all.'

I sit a few moments more staring out the windscreen. I feel a sense of needing to explain to him. Needing to let him in in some way. Needing to let him know how grateful I am for all he is doing for me. Have I even properly thanked him? I can't remember. But I can't think of the right words to do any of this.

All I manage to say is 'Thanks.' I wish he could hear the rest but I'm just not capable of transmitting it yet.

I get out of the car and back into my apartment. I suddenly feel overwhelmingly exhausted, so I go straight to bed.

Chapter 46

Arthur wants to try and identify what might have led me down this path given I wasn't always like this. I used to live what you may term a normal life with a normal mind. Nothing to make me stand out as peculiar to others.

Somewhere in my twenties things started to change. It's hard to pinpoint as I didn't simply wake up one morning with all these new bizarre thoughts running through my brain. I wasn't suddenly introduced one day to this higher force that had taken over my brain assuring me it was here to save me.

It sneaked in gradually. Perhaps it was busy with other brains so couldn't commit to giving me its full attention straight away. It just occasionally appeared and then disappeared again. Almost unnoticeable, and certainly ignorable at first.

Arthur asks if I have ever actually been seriously ill. Given my fears this seems a sensible place to start. I know where he is going with this and have already arrived at the conclusion myself in the past as it does present as a somewhat logical explanation. If the notion of logic can even be applied to this realm which is perhaps a stretch.

'I did spend some time in hospital. I went in for a routine operation but there were some complications and I didn't seem to recover in a way that was expected. I was not at death's door or anything, but neither was I very well. After a few days I became aware of being labelled a special case. I remember trainee doctors coming to observe me, and I would overhear hushed conversations discussing my seemingly strange reaction.'

'That must have been scary for you.'

'I don't think I paid all that much attention to it at the time. Days passed and I eventually showed signs of recovery and was discharged. But I guess some things maybe stuck in my head. The main one being that I don't have a body that copes well.'

'So, you feel you need to protect yourself from getting ill. More so than others might.'

'I guess so, maybe. It was never one big rush of fear that suddenly engulfed me though from the moment I left the hospital. It seemed more to creep up in some sort of slow delayed reaction. I went back to my normal life and nothing really changed at first.'

'Do you remember when you first noticed things change?'

'Not really no. I think I started taking more care with washing my hands after touching things but sort of told myself this was just common sense and I should have been doing it all along. Then over time I realised I was avoiding things because I thought it was the safer option than to put myself in an environment of potential danger. I just followed along with all these new instructions my brain was giving me and didn't give it too much thought at first. But then I became aware of it starting to really impact my life.'

'In what ways has it impacted your life?'

'Well, the avoiding mainly. Not just avoiding touching an object but avoiding participating in things. I've missed so many social occasions because it gets built up into too stressful a prospect in my mind. Sometimes it's even worse than missing social occasions. It's missing full days because I simply can't convince my brain it's safe to leave my home.'

'That must be very hard for you.'

'It's as though I'm looking out at a life that exists, but I'm not allowed to participate in it. The life I'm looking at appears to be fun, yet my brain is telling me there is all this invisible danger. So, every day I feel scared. Every day I feel exhausted.

When I stop and acknowledge this, I am then often joined by overwhelming sadness.'

'Which is when the depression appears?'

'Yes. I feel some level of sadness accompany me through all my days, but it is sort of functioning sadness if that makes sense. I still manage to leave the house and go to work. Then there are periods though where it takes over. It doesn't seem content to just sit on the side lines, so it pushes its way in and pulls me down. It's so wearing living in an almost continual state of fear. I feel so tired all the time. This, combined with realisations of all the things I'm missing out on, drain me of any enthusiasm to want to keep going.'

He looks at me with compassion and moves the box of tissues a little further to my side of the table.

Chapter 47

I continue on with my weekly visits to Arthur. Talking about what has been going on feels strange and amazing and scary and light and dark all at the same time. I have never voiced these words before to anyone, and aside from all this mixture of emotions something is also telling me it's a good thing to get these words out.

Each visit is different.

There are times when I simply sit and cry the whole time and barely manage any coherent words at all. The ever-present sadness in my daily life has found its biggest audience and wants to show off in front of Arthur.

There are times when I struggle to think of things to say. His questions are met with short answers. I can't seem to grasp hold of the necessary detail to expand. He will stay silent, patiently waiting for me to find this detail. All this does is make me uncomfortable because I know I'm not capable of productively speaking on this day. I find myself wanting to plead with him 'please say some more words because I seem to have run out.'

There are times when I can't stop talking. Almost as though it is suddenly making so much more sense when said aloud. I need to keep the momentum going in order to finally reach some kind of full and proper understanding.

I hope that all these variations of visits are helpful or leading towards something else that is helpful. I never feel quite sure what is correct. Is there even a correct?

Arthur doesn't seem phased by any of them though. He just sits patiently allowing me to be how I seem to need to be that week. I guess he just works with what he's got. Perhaps he views all as valid parts of this process.

I eventually decide to choose that same view and not dwell too much on it.

I suspect I will be visiting Arthur for a long time yet anyway so it could end up a little monotonous if every visit was the same experience.

One thing that does stay the same in every visit is that Nathan drives me there and back. And waits outside in his car the whole entire time. I'm not sure if he's still worried that I will try and make some kind of escape, or he just wants to be close in case for some reason I need him.

Either way, the more he turns up for me the more I am touched by his kindness.

His continual checking on me was irritating at first. But now I almost look forward to his messages. I can't quite understand why he's doing all this for me. It's surprising to me.

One day I find myself smiling at a funny message he has sent me. His messages have often been infused with humour which has up until now been wasted on me, but today I appear to be having a different reaction.

The emptiness I've been existing in has accepted a small visitor. It's not overly recognisable but I think it might in some small vague way resemble happiness.

It prompts me to reject my autopilot response of 'I'm fine' that he is usually graced with. Instead I attempt at engaging in his humour. It's likely a subpar attempt but at least my brain wants to do something different.

He responds immediately and I can almost feel his delight bursting through the words. We go back and forth a little in the same vein and it's nice.

This is how we used to be. I realise how much I've missed it.

Chapter 48

I notice more and more of these small little improvements over the coming days and one day I find myself looking out the window feeling the desire to go outside.

I have of course been outside to attend therapy appointments, but no other attempts have even been remotely considered up until this moment.

The sun is out. I think it has been out quite a lot recently, but I have rejected its attempts to lure me to it. Today is different though. I feel a wave of need to be in its company.

I get dressed and stand at the front door. Don't think too much Amy. Just do it.

I take a few slow steps beyond my door then stand completely still for a little time. It feels so bright. My eyes need time to adjust. The light breeze swaying around me feels strange but nice.

I feel the encouraging warmth of the sun on my skin and eventually take some more steps forward.

I have no plan for where I'm walking to but maybe I don't need to be walking to anywhere. I just need to be walking. To be outside. With the air, and with the sun. It feels good.

The road my apartment is on is quite long, so I walk in the same direction for a while. Once I reach the end I turn onto a much busier road. I almost immediately realise I've made a mistake. I should have walked in the other direction. It's loud. Cars driving. There are people. Not many, but they seem to be talking loudly. They feel too near me, even though they are on the opposite side of the road.

I turn around and go back home, this time walking faster.

Later in the day I decide to call Nathan and tell him. I know he will appreciate knowing I made an attempt at least to leave the house on my own.

'That's great!'

'But I wasn't outside for very long, I had to come straight back after freaking out.'

'Don't think too much about how long you managed outside, or the fact you freaked out. Those things are completely normal given this was your first time. The important thing is that you felt like you wanted to, and you followed through.'

'Ok.'

'Trust me Ames, you should be proud of yourself. I certainly am.'

I think about his words. This seems a strange thing to be proud of. Not exactly high up there on a list of life's greatest achievements. Unlikely even on the list at all. But I concede I have a very different list of achievements to focus on at the moment.

'Thanks.'

'Do you want to maybe try again tomorrow? I could come with you. We could drive out somewhere quiet and have a walk in the countryside if that's maybe easier?'

'I'm not sure.'

'Have a think about it. It doesn't have to be tomorrow. It can be the day after, or the day after that. You just name the day and I will be there.'

'Ok, I will think about it and let you know.'

'Great.' He pauses before thoughtfully adding, 'You're going to get through this Ames, I promise you.'

We end the call and I think about his suggestion. A walk in the countryside does actually sound quite appealing. I wouldn't have to worry too much about noise or other people, and I could get to spend more time with the sun.

I don't commit to any decisions but in this current moment I am feeling drawn to taking Nathan up on his offer.

It's a few more days before I feel like acting on it though. He appears on my doorstep not long after I've sent him a message to confirm. I presume he (correctly) senses that I can't have too much time to think about this or will likely change my mind.

We drive for about an hour and it's nice to be in his company.

It's a bright sunny day (otherwise I would not have agreed) and Nathan has picked a beautiful quiet spot for us to walk.

We pass the occasional dog walker, but we are pretty much alone aside from that.

Nathan does two things which I am extremely grateful for.

He doesn't keep asking me if I'm ok.

And, he keeps the conversation light with no reference to my current situation.

I need this break. Out here on this walk I'm going to pretend to be normal. Just for these couple of hours I'm simply walking in the countryside catching up with a friend.

I've tried to wrap my brain in numerous invisible plasters to allow for this pretence. They will of course fall off again soon but for this short time they will hopefully hold, allowing some resemblance of mental stability.

Nathan fills me in on what's been happening at work. New projects that are causing stress. New clients that are also causing stress (but of course still being assessed for his potential soul mate status). His stories keep me amused and I feel a rush of warmth for him.

He senses when I grow a little quieter that it might be time to take me home and doesn't make any big deal out of it. He simply guides us back to the car and drives me home.

I'm about to get out of the car when I pause before opening the door. I'm not quite sure what I want to say. I turn to look at him and try and will appropriate sentences to form in my brain. The only words I manage to actually voice though are, 'Thank you'. He deserves so many more, but it seems he will have to wait a bit longer.

'Any time.' He responds with a smile.

Chapter 49

Over the next few weeks we repeat this country walking quite a few times. I find myself looking forward to it. I wasn't entirely convinced I was any longer capable of looking forward to things, so this I know is a very significant step in progress.

One day we are walking, and it feels important to share with Nathan.

'I think I might be getting better.' This statement feels precariously close to tempting fate, so I quickly add, 'A little bit anyway.'

'You definitely are.' He smiles. 'Not just because you are making it out of the house. I see it in you.'

I smile. 'I think I see it in me too. Or rather I feel it. I feel something changing.'

'You have no idea how relieved I am to hear you say that.' I look at his face and I see this relief exuding from his expression.

We walk in silence for a little while before I say, 'You have been so amazing to me Nathan, I know I don't deserve such a good friend as you. When I think now about everything you've done, I can't quite believe it.'

'You'd do the same for me.'

Would I? Maybe before.

He continues, 'You really scared me there for a while. I couldn't just sit and watch you struggle and fade. No way was I ever going to let that happen.'

'I'm sorry I scared you.'

'I know you didn't have much choice in the matter.'

'No, I don't think I did. But still. I am sorry.'

'I know Ed leaving was tough on you. I suspect this maybe would have happened regardless though. But I'm still going to say this to you – Ed was not your only friend. I know Sal has a funny way of showing it sometimes, but she does really care about you. And you have been really missed by a lot of people in the office. So many have been asking me how you are doing and when you will be back. These people are your friends Ames, don't go forgetting that ok?'

'I know.' Do I know? I never really seem able to fully grasp that someone might want to be my friend when I behave so terribly sometimes.

I continue, 'You are right about Ed leaving being tough. I really miss him. But I always thought this was the best thing for him. I am happy for him.'

I do miss Ed, but I think his part in contributing to my recent state was more than just feeling like I have lost another friend. He represented yet another person able to take on fun exciting adventures I knew I myself couldn't even hope to attempt. He was engaging in life as it should be. I have not been allowed to engage for so long, it often cuts deeply when I see how easy it is for others.

I watched him move on with his life, leaving me behind in the suffocating bubble I always feel left in.

'He's been in touch a few times. I've rolled out some quite impressive excuses for why you haven't been contactable but I'm not sure how much longer they will hold. So, if you don't want him suddenly appearing on your doorstep, I'd say now is the time to get in touch with him.'

'I will. So, you didn't tell him what's been going on?'

'No, I didn't. I thought about it, but we both know he would have been straight on the next flight back here to be by your side. I just didn't really think that would help anyone. I hope I made the right decision.'

'You did. You absolutely did. He needs to focus on his life in Singapore.'

'And you need to focus on your life here. And I am nominating myself as the person to help you do that. Given the fact I am not allowing any other candidates to nominate themselves, and also given the fact we are not in love with each other like you and Ed were, I conclude I have successfully been granted the position.'

'Well, you have been proving yourself to be quite skilled in the position already, so I'd be honoured to have you continue.' I smile before continuing. 'And for the record, Ed and I were not in love with each other.'

'Hmm... maybe not you. But I'm almost certain there were inappropriate feelings on his side. But we're not going to dwell on that. Thankfully Singapore stepped in and stopped things from getting too messy, so we can say a little thank you to Singapore and move you along with your life here.'

I smile again. 'Sounds good.'

Chapter 50

My life does move along.

Arthur has started me on a specific recommended therapy process called Cognitive Behavioural Therapy (or CBT as we refer to it given acronyms are well liked in this realm). He assures me it can be very effective in the tackling of OCD. I can't attest yet to that effectiveness as it unfortunately involves some period of time before results can be noticed. I am hopeful, however, given his assurances on it.

It is hard work. It's not simply confined to the hour time slot I spend with Arthur. It's something that needs to be worked on every day as it essentially involves training my brain to think in a different way. Given it has been allowed to think in a destructive way for such a long period of time, it's going to take some real effort to retrain it. But retrain it I absolutely must.

I think talking to Arthur in general,

however, has been good for me. This, likely in combination with the medication, seems to direct me towards eventually feeling able to attempt going back to work.

I have miraculously managed to still keep my job throughout this time. Or more accurately put, Nathan has kept it for me. He managed to convince them to hire a freelancer to cover my work temporarily. I barely registered this kindness back when he originally told me this plan. I barely registered any of his words so there was little hope of registering the beauty in his actions.

Now it is my first day back and I'm so incredibly grateful to him. I'm not sure I could have coped with having to find a new job right now.

I actually feel something resembling excitement at the prospect of getting back into work. It's been so long since I've felt this feeling so I can't be entirely sure. Maybe it's nervousness. Or maybe a bit of both. Whatever it is, it gets me out of the house successfully so I'm content to feel it.

I've always enjoyed my job, but my interest fell away when everything else fell away. It seems to be finding its way back to me now though which is a very relieving thing to acknowledge.

My first day back passes with air around me that feels filled with kindness. Everyone I see tells me how nice it is to see me back. Most I'm sure don't know the reason I was off – they perhaps assume illness, or a bereavement but everyone is too polite to ask. They just treat me like I was only on an extended holiday. They are good people here. I am genuinely feeling a little joy in this day.

And the next day. And the next day. It feels really good to be back.

At the end of my first week back I am making my way to the elevators to leave for the day when I see Ben. He spots me at the same time and a beaming smile immediately appears on his face.

'Amy! What are you doing here? Are you back working here? I thought you'd left. I asked around but nobody seemed to be too sure. Has everything been ok?'

I smile at his slightly manic question firing.

'Yes, I'm back. I just had to take some time off to deal with some personal stuff but I'm definitely still working here.'

'Great! Good to hear. I mean, no, sorry, not good to hear you had some stuff going on but good you're back.' He pauses before adding, 'I'm rambling a bit here aren't I, sorry.'

I laugh. 'It's fine. It's very sweet of you to notice I wasn't around. So, how have you been?'

'Good, good. Busy with work as usual. There have been a lot of late nights recently while we work towards this big proposal coming up.'

'That must be tough on the new relationship.'

'New relationship?'

'Yeh, you're seeing someone aren't you?'

'Oh. Yes. Or rather, yes, I was, but it didn't work out unfortunately. She was nice enough but we both could see we weren't the best match, so rather than drag it out we parted as friends. All very civilized.'

'Great. I mean, great that it was civilized, not great you had to break up.' I manage to stop there as I think I'm about to catch his waffling.

'How about you? Can I ask about the ex?'

'The ex?'

'Yeh, your ex you told me you were still in love with. Any update on that situation?'

Oh. I forgot I'd used that excuse.

Ok. Two choices Amy. Continue the lie and things will stay the same. Or. Believe you're changing and might be able to actually manage this and tell Ben the truth. Not the full truth obviously. It's not really an appropriate time to throw that all out there whilst we're stood in front of the office elevators. Just the truth about being single and available and not in love with anyone else.

'I think he's pretty much out the picture now.'

'And, is anyone else in the picture? Did I miss my window of opportunity?' He smiles.

I return his smile. 'No, no one else.'

'So, if I were to ask you out for a second date might that be something you would consider?'

My smile beams brighter and I answer, 'It might be.'

I don't know if I'm really going to be able to do this. But I do know that I actually feel able to try now and that has never even been a notion before. It's small progress but small progress I am aware is the way this works. I can't expect big changes overnight. Or even over a handful of nights. This is going to take a long time.

Maybe Ben won't wait. Maybe I will run before he's given the chance to wait. But what's appeared in this moment are things I thought I had lost forever. Feelings of untainted happiness, feelings of hope, and feelings of strength in ability to try.

I'm really actually able and willing to try.

We step into the elevator together and as the doors close, I catch a glimpse of Ed's old desk and smile.

Printed in Great Britain
by Amazon